HER

ROYAL

HAREM

THE COMPLETE REVERSE HAREM SERIES

N.J. ADEL

This is a work of fiction. Names, characters, businesses, places, events, and incidents either are the products of the author's imagination or used in a fictitious manner. Any resemblance to actual persons, living or dead, or actual events is purely coincidental..

Published by N.J. Adel with Salacious Queen Publishing

Email us at N.J.adel.majesty@gmail.com
ISBN: 9781095023624

WARNING: THIS BOOK FEATURES EXPLICIT DEPICTIONS OF SEX AND OTHER MATERIAL THAT MAY OFFEND SOME AUDIENCES. THEREFORE, IS INTENDED FOR ADULTS ONLY. SOME OR ALL OF THE **BDSM** SCENES MIGHT BE **EXTREME** AND ARE **NOT TO BE TRIED** WITHOUT THE NECESSARY EXPERIENCE AND TRUST.

ALL CHARACTERS DEPICTED ARE OVER THE AGE OF 18.

TABLE OF CONTENTS

Also by N.J. Adel

Reverse Harem Standalones
All the Teacher's Pet Beasts
All the Teacher's Little Belles
All the Teacher's Bad Boys
All the Teacher's Valentines (Sweeter than
Chocolate Anthology Novella)

Fantasy Reverse Harem
Seratis the Goddess of Egypt
Seratis Daughter of the Sun
Seratis War of the Gods

Dark MC and Mafia Romance
I Hate You then I Love You Collection
Darkness Between Us
Nine Minutes Later
Nine Minutes Xtra
Nine Minutes Forever

Contemporary Romance
The Italian Heartthrob

PART 1

HER MAJESTY'S HAREM

CHAPTER 1

I wish I could see their eyes.

The way they squeeze shut. How they roll back.

But they're always blindfolded.

For my own safety, of course.

I lean back, my palms resting on my bed silky sheets, as the lineup starts.

Escorted by an army of guards, twenty men enter my room one by one. Eyes, asses and cocks covered in black.

I'm supposed to look at them. Ogle to take my pick for tonight. Instead, I look, from the corner of my eyes, at the guard standing next to me.

Quinn. One of my two personal escorts.

His eyes are dark clouds, his fleshy mouth tight, his posture rigid, just like every night I crave more than my own touch.

I glance at the other side. At Ed. The blonde version of Quinn. His expression and stance aren't much different either.

I smile.

Then I amble toward the half-naked…servers. "Are you all here by consent?"

"Yes, Your Majesty." Their voices boom as one. Not a good sign. Someone has coached them.

"I do not like men who lie." I stand a few inches in front of them, my body itching to get rid of the robe covering it. "If you're here because you're afraid or someone has promised you something in return, speak now, and you shall go unharmed," I say, and three swallow. "The same applies if you have a change of heart." Five have sweaty foreheads now. I pause, but no one makes a sound. "But if you don't speak, and I discover you're lying, you will not leave in one piece."

Murmurs and gasps fill the room.

"Those who wish to leave, please step forward," Quinn says, his voice eager. I know he wishes they all would.

But only eight do.

CHAPTER 2

I approach the first of the twelve men dying to please me. As my fingers caress his chiseled chest, I whisper in his ear, "What's your name?"

"Sean, Your Majesty."

My hands slide down to his hard abs, and they clench in response. I rest my chin on his shoulder and look at my two protectors. "What am I doing to you now, Sean?"

"Your Majesty is…touching me." He chuckles, his arms moving nervously.

"Where?"

"On my chest and my abdomen."

My palms swipe backwards and press against his ass. "And now?"

"My…ass." His voice shakes, and I enjoy the growing bulge in his underwear and the glares of Quinn and Ed.

"Do you want to touch me, too?"

"Yes! So much." His hands ball into fists. "But I know better."

Everything about him begs to differ. The rules are clear. No fucking. No coming. No touching me. Not without permission. My permission.

I step away. "I don't think you do, Sean."

"Oh, Majesty, please. I—"

"Silence," I warn him, and he bows his head, sighing in regret. "Practice your self-control, boy, and come back in a few weeks. Maybe then."

"Thank you, Majesty."

CHAPTER 3

I skip the two next to Sean. I have no interest in weight-lifters tonight. Muscles are good, but nothing too bulging.

Next in line, a blond model.

I stare at his mouth and lean body. Delicious. "Name?"

"Camden, Your Majesty."

I slide my thumb across his full lips. Soft and warm. Pictures of them whispering dirty words and suckling my tits make my pussy throb. "I'm going to kiss you now, Camden."

"It's my honor." He swallows, and his lips part as I bend him to mine.

A man who knows what he's doing. I like that. His kiss, the right amount of lips, teeth and tongue, sends a fresh gush down my pussy, and I have the sudden urge to press myself against his cock.

I do just that. "God, you're hard."

His gasps scorch my face, and he clasps his hands behind his back.

Good boy.

I stroke his erection, and he moans. The other men's breathing goes higher as their faces redden, and their dicks stir.

Having several men in the same room turned on only by my voice and unseen gestures, unafraid to show their lust, makes me wet as fuck.

I lay my hand on Camden's heart and bite his earlobe, whispering, "I want to fuck you so hard."

His chest heaves as his teeth stab his lips. "I'm all yours, Majesty. I know the rules, but you're the Queen. Your Majesty can do whatever you want with my body."

Wrong.

Unlike what others might think, the Queen can't do however she pleases.

I can have any man in the kingdom, let them satisfy whatever whim or desire obsesses me, as long as they can't see, and as long as they're not inside me. Who knows what they might do when they see their ruler's nakedness? How far they can stay under control? Or later, when they go back to their mundane lives, what stories they might tell, even to themselves?

Fucking commoners is simply too dangerous. Playing with them while my guards watch, though...

I grin at the thought. "I wish I could, but for now... Tits or pussy?"

"Oh God," he says under his breath, his heart banging his chest. "Whichever pleases Your Majesty more."

"Fuck, Camden. You were doing so well." I pucker my lips in disappointment. "Shame. Now you can have neither."

"What?" His head jerks. "Why, Majesty?"

"I gave you a choice, and you didn't seize the opportunity. What does that say about you?"

He shakes his head rapidly. "Pussy. Definitely, pussy."

"Too late."

"I'm sorry, Majesty. Please. May I, at least, come back next time?"

"Hesitation is not a quality I appreciate in a man." I nod at one the guards who escorted the men. "You may not."

Camden growls as he's guided outside the room.

CHAPTER 4

I move to the next man. A soldier. Over six feet. Cropped, black hair. Dark skin. Long legs. And by his ass and the outline of his semi-hard cock, I'd say this one is a bad boy. "I hope you don't let me down tonight, sir. I have a thing for men who serve." I spin, lifting my eyes to my personal escorts. They both sigh.

"I'm honored to serve Your Majesty in any way possible."

"Being here means you're no longer in my army. What happened?"

"Exempted by Royal Decree. I lost two brothers and a kidney in the last war. Your Majesty's kindness can never be matched."

A war hero. Am I drooling? "Sorry for your loss. I bet you can use some cheering up."

He gives a shy smile, and I can't help but taste his lips. My eyes dip to his cock. The tint against the fabric is driving me insane. I go behind him and explore his firm ass. Then I slide underneath the black cotton and squeeze him. The throbbing in my sex is now painful.

I stretch on my toes to reach his ear. "Tits

or pussy…sir?"

He lets out a heavy breath. "If it's my choice, it will be pussy. I want to taste Your Majesty come apart."

"Excellent choice. I want to come apart for you too, sir." My fist feels his length, and he groans. "But first you have to answer two questions. Would you die for me, sir?"

"In a heartbeat, Majesty," he says softly, his breaths catching.

"I know you would, sir. But would you lose your cock for me?"

He gasps. "I…I don't think I would, Majesty."

I stop touching him and move to see his face. He blanches. His lashes are fluttering behind the blindfold, and his mouth is tight.

"Why is that, sir?"

"I don't want to live half a man. And one day, I want to have a woman and a family of my own."

"I see. Thank you for your candor. You shall be rewarded, sir." I press my body to his steaming one as I grab his hands. "You can feel me up, soldier."

A chorus of moans erupts.

The soldier's jaw drops, and his hands shake a little. "Yes?"

"Um-hum. Take off my robe."

His calloused fingers find my neck and slowly feel my shoulders under the silk. His chest heaves as he travels down to my tits. He circles them with gossamer pressure, and I swallow. My juice trickles between my thighs, our breaths loud and sharp as the robe finds the floor and his hands are squeezing me.

"Oh, sir, you're hungry…and not shy at all."

The lip-biting and the other seven hard-ons satisfy me. I kiss the soldier again as he has one palm on my tit and the other on my ass. "Know your territory, soldier."

His fingertips tease my hips before they slip between my thighs. His thumb finds my clit, moving in circles. Then he slides his middle finger inside my pussy. "Your Majesty is drenched." His hand presses my tit harder as he slides a second finger in me, moaning.

I smirk, and then look to the side, at the man standing next to him. He's shifting on his legs, chewing on his lips, barely containing his lustful sounds, his hands clasped over his crotch. I take one of his hands, and he jumps. "It's okay. It's me."

His lips twitch with a smile as his hands drop, revealing a massive erection. Even bigger than the soldier's. I stroke him under his underwear as the soldier fucks me with his fingers. "You shall give me a pearl necklace, boy."

He nods, his dirty blond hair falling forward covering his forehead, his mouth open, lost for words.

I pick another man and order the rest away. "My whole body is primed. I'm ready to go."

CHAPTER 5

I lie on my bed while Quinn and Ed undress the three men and give them a final inspection. Who knows what they could be hiding? Despite how meticulous the selection process is, some lunatics still find their way in.

My protectors guide the soldier to where my legs part and the other two to either side of me. I push the back of both their heads, leading their mouths to my tits. Their tongues circle around my nipples, which are now hard as pebbles. Then they suckle with their full, wet mouths, their grunts low and sexy, and my core is soaking.

I take in the three naked bodies and the three big, fat cocks surrounding me, standing at attention for me. I stare at Quinn and Ed. Their eyes are blazing with fury, jealousy and lust, and I can barely stand the throbbing in my cunt. My gaze travels down to their pants, and even though their hands are set before their groins, I see the bulges of their aching dicks.

"You can eat my pussy now, sir," I say

between breaths.

The soldier crouches and devours me. His tongue swirls among my folds, while the two on my side suckle my tits. A heavy pressure gathers down my belly. "Oh God, I want to come so badly. Fuck me with your fingers, soldier."

As the soldier's two long fingers go in and out of me, and his mouth continues to fuck me, I wrap my palms around the boys' cocks. They both tremble, pre-cum hot on my fingers.

"I wish I could fuck you." I look at Quinn, and then at Ed. "I wish I could fuck both of you."

They grimace, and they both mouth "me too."

I moan. "All three of you, touch me now."

Now I have six hands hungrily roaming every inch of my body, two hard cocks in my hands, a soldier fucking my brains out. My breaths snag and come shakily. "Boys…when you hear me scream…come on my tits."

They groan as my back arches and my lips part with successive screams of pleasure. Then I shudder as the soldier drinks me in and the boys' cum drips sticky and hot on my chest, and my dearest escorts' tormented eyes are all I see.

PART 2

HER MAJESTY & THE VIRGINS

1.
HER MAJESTY

The masseuse's fingers work on my shoulders and back, memories of last night with the blindfolded men, and many nights before, washing over me.

Not enough.

What I have with them is not enough. Never has been. Never will be.

I do love their pleasing touches. My control over their bodies.

Over them.

But I want to see it in their eyes. The wreck. The pain. The surrender.

When a man is making love to a woman, it's not about what his cock does to her. It's about how he feels when his cock is in her. What's better than eyes to show feelings?

And I can't have either: cocks or eyes.

I want more.

Much more than coming off to a bunch of men who are eager to serve their Queen with hands and tongues.

I get off the table, and the maids put me in an off-shoulder, blue gown that matches the red shades of my hair perfectly. Then Quinn comes in.

The flicker of admiration in his gray eyes lightens my mood, before it's buried behind the soldier look he's been wearing for a decade.

"Good morning, Sir Quinlan." *You look good today, too.*

I always love his long, black hair when it bounces off his shoulders as he walks like this.

"Good morning, Majesty." He bows. "High Priest has arrived."

"Let's not keep him waiting then. Dispensation Day is one of my favorite days of the month."

2.
QUINN

With Her Majesty, it is all about consent. She never coerces. Always gives a choice.

That's why we have Dispensation Day and why—despite her…flaws—she's loved. By the people.

By me.

I stand next to her as she sits in the throne, unable to tell her how ravishing she looks this morning.

How ravishing she looks every day.

How her sweet smell is driving me—

"High Priest Buchannan!" the herald announces.

The Temple High Priest leads the apprentices who no longer wish to devote their lives to religion into the throne room. Nine boys and three girls shuffle toward us, their eyes on their feet.

"Majesty." High Priest bows.

She inches a brow. "Twelve this month? Please tell me the number of the devotees is higher."

He clears his throat. "Fifteen, Your Majesty."

"Almost half of your students want to leave, High Priest. What does that say about you and your operation?"

"I—"

"Silence." Her index finger brushes against her lips. "I'll process the girls first." She motions for them to step forward.

When they do, Her Majesty asks them how long they've been in the Temple and why they've decided to leave. The answers are almost always the same. When they hit puberty, their families send them to become devotees. After a few months, they realize it's never been what they want to do with their lives. Never will be.

Especially, if they've fallen in love, like these three girls. Abstinence is no longer a possibility.

Still, they try and try to please their families, to please God, but when they fail, they impatiently wait for their Dispensation Day. The day they turn eighteen and come here to tell Her Majesty about their plans and dreams. Convince her they're leaving the Temple for good reason.

"Which of these handsome gentlemen are

yours?" Her Majesty asks.

The girls point at their lovers, and the Queen allows the Temple boys to approach. "I presume the three couples have consummated their love already?"

The kids blush, as if on cue.

Her Majesty gasps. "Naughty little ones."

They mumble incoherent pleas, and she gestures for them to shut up. Then her laugh rings in the room. "Rest, I'm not High Priest. Young love is a refreshing notion, not a disappointing sin. But what will disappoint me is you boys not having plans for your future with these beautiful ladies."

"We do Your Majesty," one of the boys says. He then elaborates how his skills are better used in carpentry and raves about all the efforts he's willing to make to be with the girl he loves. The others follow his lead.

"I'm convinced. Each of you will be sent to the right faction to hone your skills for a trial period of three months. After you've proven your merit, you shall have my permission and blessing to pursue your happily ever after."

A chorus of "Thank you, Your Majesty" flares in the room. Then the Queen dismisses them and calls for the other six boys.

One by one they speak of their dream professions, and she grants them their wishes.

A painter. A farmer. A soldier. A blacksmith. A poet. Then the last of them approaches. A well-built boy with black hair and arctic blue eyes.

"Ah, look at you. You're taller than Sir Quinlan already. Let me guess, you wish to be a soldier, or is it the Royal Guards you hope to join?" she asks.

"I'm afraid not, Your Majesty."

"Is that so? What is your plan then?"

"I'm sorry to disappoint you, Your Majesty, but I don't have a plan. I simply don't wish to be a priest. I'm not a fighter either."

"Then what are you?"

"I wish I knew. I haven't developed a certain passion for any trade, and my skills are too mediocre to excel at any."

She grimaces. "You know I can't let you break the commitment you made to the Temple unless you have a convincing reason. If it's not a different profession or affection you seek…"

The boy kneels at her feet, his hands clasped in supplication, lifting his beseeching eyes to her face. "I beg you, Majesty. Please don't send me back. There must be another way I can serve Your Majesty and the kingdom. I don't know what it is, but there must be something."

"Such a waste. A fine man like you, lost, unable to find his passion in life." She sighs and takes his hand between hers. "But never worry. We shall find your true calling. You're too good-looking to be a priest anyway."

My hands clench into fists.

The boy grins and kisses her hand. "I'm forever in debt to your kindness, Your Majesty."

"I'm pondering initiating a new faction just for boys with your…qualities. But first you must answer one question truthfully."

"Of course."

"Come closer. This might be something you don't want to disclose in public."

He stands and bends his head for her to whisper in his ear. When she does, he blushes, his lips twitching with a smile. Then he gazes at her and nods.

A surge of anger travels through me as my eyes dip to his crotch and see how his pants fit a little tighter now.

She gives him a familiar look I wish I'd never see again for the rest of my life.

Unless it's for…

Me.

Go ahead. Judge me all you want. I know it's wrong. Forbidden.

She's my Queen, and I'm her personal

escort. Her protector. I'm not allowed to have feelings for her. To want her. To lie with her every night in my head. To be so jealous I contemplate snapping this boy in half.

But I love her. With all my heart. There's nothing I can do to change that.

I've loved her since the day I stood like these boys, and she allowed me to join the Royal Guards. The day I stood one pace from her, my lips touching her hand in gratitude, wondering if her hand was that soft how her mouth would feel. I was so afraid she'd notice what her smell, and even her lightest touch, did to my dick. Back then, I was a kid and knew nothing of Her Majesty's...salaciousness.

Now I know not only did she notice, she enjoyed it too. Just like she does at the moment with the boy.

"Thank you, High Priest. Please see the gentlemen to their new factions. As for..." She smirks at the boy.

"Theodore, Your Majesty," he says.

"As for Theodore, he is to reside and work at the palace until further notice. You may all be dismissed."

***

I walk by Her Majesty's side to her chambers, questions banging in my head until they force themselves on my tongue. "Majesty, if I may ask, the new faction you mentioned, what is it? And what question did the boy have to answer to join?"

She smirks. "You may not."

"Majesty, with all due respect, I'm in charge of your safety." I lower my voice. "You must know the boy was *aroused* by whatever you said to him, and if I could see that, High Priest might have seen it, too. This could quickly turn into a threat to Your Majesty's reign. We do everything in our might to keep your…adventures a secret and stifle any rumors before they even start. Flirting with a boy half your age in public is—"

"You've crossed a line, Sir Quinlan." She stops and stares at me. "The next time you speak to me that way, you'll be released from your duties. Do you understand?"

She hasn't called me Sir Quinlan in private in years. And releasing me from my duties? I bite my cheek, my blood simmering. "Yes, Majesty."

As she continues to her room, I follow. Edward is standing by the door. When we reach him, she summons both of us inside. I close the door behind me and take my place before my Queen.

"Majesty seems troubled," Edward says. "Something went wrong with Dispensation today?"

"You mean you don't know? I thought news traveled faster around here." She narrows her eyes as she takes a seat. "Fill him in, Sir Quinlan."

Again with that. "Her Majesty has taken quite an interest in a Temple boy that she'd start a new faction just for his sake." A burning sensation whips in my stomach. "She's even allowed him to reside at the palace without the proper investigations required for giving anyone such privilege."

"Jealous much?" she teases.

"This is not…about me," I lie. "Having a complete stranger wandering around the palace is not protocol."

"Then investigate. He's on a three-month trial period like the rest, which means he'll be monitored the whole time. It's not like he's granted unlimited access to the palace."

"And so we shall, Majesty," Edward says before I can respond, his arms folded across his chest.

That's it. He's not even curious about her intentions for that boy? How can he control himself like that? As if we aren't in the same boat?

Yes, he, too, loves her. Worships her.

Who wouldn't?

Wars have been started for her. To have her. Yet no one has won her. I dare any man in our position not to fall for her. Being this close to her beauty, her power, is overwhelming.

Our Queen. Our downfall.

She burns us every time she fools around under our noses, playing and using men like toys, rubbing it in our faces. My only consolation is that she never allows a man inside her. The hope that if she ever does, it will be…

"I trust Theodore is going to be *safe* in the palace?" she demands.

"Of course, Majesty," Edward replies, and my nostrils flare.

"If he mysteriously disappears or breaks his neck in an accident, I'll hold you both accountable."

"Understood." He takes a deep breath, his jaws tight.

"Thank you, Ed. I suggest you teach your friend something about manners." She looks at me. "You see how Ed never crosses a line even though jealousy is ripping him apart on the inside?" She switches her gaze toward him, a charming smile on her face, and stretches her hand for him to kiss it.

His reward.

He closes his eyes and takes his time as his lips brush against the back of her hand.

Seldom do I get jealous of Edward; we're brothers in arms, and we share everything—even the heartache every night we have to watch her naked with some fucker's tongue in her cunt while we can't even touch her.

Except for moments like these; when she favors him for being her obedient pet, flames eat my heart.

Would she, at least, punish me for misbehaving? Her punishment is a reward in itself. It means she's not ignoring me. It means she cares.

"Dismissed," she orders.

No.

I bow my head and start for the door, dragging my self-loathing thoughts with me.

"Not so fast, Sir Quinlan," she says. "I'm not done with you."

I smile.

3.
HER MAJESTY

Quinn wheels back to me, the doors shut with a loud thud as Ed exits. "Majesty."

"You misbehaved today."

"I know. I'm very sorry," he murmurs as he bows his head.

"An apology is not enough. You must be punished," I speak slowly, in a tone I know is driving him insane.

My loyal protector. My eternal salve.

I rise and walk around him. He swallows, his breath catching. "Kneel."

His knees touch the marble tiles.

I sit on the edge of my bed, leaving him like this for five minutes. He doesn't move or look up.

"Look at me," I finally say.

He tilts his face up, and I see his beautiful, tortured, gray eyes.

"Disarm, take off your coat and shirt, and crawl to me."

He removes his sword and shrugs off the

leather coat. Slowly, his fingers untie his black shirt and work off the buttons one by one.

I stare.

Quinn's build is exactly my taste. Tall. Lean. Big, muscular arms with thick sinews along them. Broad shoulders and chest. Hard abs I'm dying to feel clench against me.

Except that I can't.

It doesn't matter if he's chiseled to perfection and I've never wanted a man more than I want him, or that his heart has never belonged to anyone but me, or that he's crawling toward my feet right now.

I can't have him.

Because I'm a fucking queen, and he's an orphan who has chosen to protect me for the rest of his life.

It doesn't change anything, though. Not about the way he feels about me or the way I...

"Take off my shoes," I command as he reaches me.

"Yes, Majesty." His hair falls over his face when he does as he's told. His touch lingers on my feet before he puts the shoes away and waits for my next words.

"Would you like to take off my stockings, too?"

"Yes, Majesty. Very much," he whispers.

I fist my hand in his hair and wrench his head back. He gasps, his eyes fixed on mine. "Because you like to touch me *very much*, don't you?"

He nods, his breaths ragged.

"But you forfeited that right a long time ago, along with the right to be jealous. Remember?"

He squeezes his eyes shut. "Yes, Majesty. I remember."

He must be recalling the night I gave him the choice. Guard me or fuck me. The first and last man I've ever offered such opportunity. And because he loves me, he chose to do the right thing. "How do you feel now?"

"Humility. Regret."

"You brought this on yourself."

"I know." His voice shakes, almost broken.

God, I want to kiss those fleshy lips and press his naked chest to mine. I want to swirl my fingers in his hair while his tongue swirls around my breasts. "Do you feel anything else?"

His lips part, but no words come out.

I yank harder at his hair. "I asked you a question."

"Yes, I do. I feel...aroused."

I release my grip, letting out a warm sigh.

"What do I do with you now?"

"Please, forgive me." He opens his eyes. "I can't help myself."

I lean forward, giving him an ample view of my cleavage. His stare eats me up, and he licks his lips. My nipples harden.

"Do you have forbidden fantasies about your Queen?"

He blinks. "Yes."

"Are you picturing one right now?"

"Yes!"

"Describe it."

"It's very inappropriate, Majesty."

The back of my neck tingles. "I still want to hear it."

He bites his lip. "I tear your clothes apart, suck your tits till they hurt, lay you on your stomach and spank your ass as my cock fucks your pussy, long and hard." His voice is intractable. Heat burns my spine.

I'll envision exactly that when I'm taking my bath, but for now I slap him.

His head whips to the side. My fingers mark his face red.

"Now, apologize and I will forgive you," I say.

He kisses my feet and my hands. "I'm sorry."

"Get up and put your clothes back on."

His shirt covers his ivory skin, and I mourn the loss of the view. "You should know I wasn't flirting with him. I only asked if he was a virgin."

He glances at me for a few seconds. "What's the purpose of such question?"

"You'll know in time."

He bows and puts on the rest of his clothes.

"Ah, Quinn…"

"Yes, Majesty?"

"You might want to adjust your dick on the way out." I laugh, knowing he's only getting harder.

4.

HER MAJESTY

In the garden, I enjoy my afternoon stroll, my beautiful guards by my side. "How long has it been since I took Theodore in?"

"Thirty days, Majesty," Ed answers.

"Great. It's time to be briefed about his progress. Send for him."

"How about we send for his superiors instead? They'd inform Your Majesty about the boy's progress much better," Quinn says.

"I've already been briefed by the butler, the kitchen master and the chief landscaper. Thank you very much. I'd like to hear from Theodore now. In fact, I'd like to see him in action. Take me to him."

He purses his lips. "Of course, Your Majesty."

We continue to the eastern side of the garden, I spot the chief landscaper and his group working on some shrubberies, while

Theodore is climbing a white foxglove tree. With no ladder, shirtless, a saw in his hand.

"Majesty." The chief bows, and his workers drop their tools and do the same.

"What's Theodore doing up there?" I stare at the boy as he climbs higher like a spider-monkey.

"Cutting some branches. Autumn is a few days away. Foxgloves shed brutally."

"Why isn't he following safety instructions? And why isn't anybody helping him?" I raise my voice.

"He doesn't look like he needs any help, Majesty. He's as strong as a stallion. As far as instructions, however; he can't seem to follow any. The boy is dumb as a brick."

"Oh, for God's sake. Even if what you claim is true, shouldn't he be at least monitored? What if he falls off the tree or that saw flies off his hand and slits *your* throat?" I stalk to the tree. "Theodore!"

His head jerks toward me, and a big smile stretches on his face. "Maje—" Abruptly, his foot slips, and he staggers before he falls on his back with a gut-wrenching thud.

My hand lifts to my mouth, stifling a gasp.

The men rush to him, but he gets up as if nothing has happened, panting, raising the saw in the air. "It's all right. I held on to it so

34

it won't fly away. God forbid it hurts anyone." He drops it with a chortle and dusts himself off.

Dear God. That's all he cares about? "But are *you* all right?"

"Oh, yes. I apologize for making a fool of myself. I was surprised to see Your Majesty again in the flesh." He bows.

I laugh. "Please clean yourself and meet me in the solarium. I'd like a word with you."

He bows again. "Majesty."

I amble back down the undulated path. "You, too, Chief."

The old man's beady eyes sink in their cavities as he bends his head. "Majesty."

***

Theodore's heels echo inside the solarium as he approaches us. He stands before me, all clean, bright sun rays from the glass doors sparkling on his wet, raven hair. The pale brown, day coat he's changed into emphasizes a physique of perfect proportions.

For the past month, I've told myself I might have exaggerated the degree of his beauty. But the clarity of those intense, blue eyes, the angularity of his brow, the carved precision of his high cheekbones…

He bows. "Majesty." His fingers comb back his hair as he straightens up and nods at my escorts. "Sir Quinlan. Sir Edward."

I rearrange the folds of my skirt, leaning against the velvet sofa I sit in, recovering from his effect on me. "How do you find your stay here, young man?"

"Marvelous. I mean…I've never dreamt of living here, even if it's for a short while."

"What's the best thing about it?"

"Uh…the food." He chuckles.

"I see." I tilt my chin up. "Do culinary arts interest you? Or do you just appreciate them?"

His gaze meets the ground. "I know I've done nothing but disappointing—"

"Don't utter that word again."

His Adam's apple bobs.

"You're a disappointment only if you believe you are so."

He raises his head. "But Your Majesty has spared nothing to help me. Allowed me the best accommodation, provided the best mentors—"

"I don't think I have. If what I saw this afternoon was how all your masters have treated you, then I owe you an apology."

Stunned, he stares at me. "It's not their fault that I'm stupid."

"Except you're not." I lift one hand up. In response, Ed opens the solarium doors and ushers the chief landscaper in.

I enjoy the morbid expression on the old man's face. "Chief, what have you called Theodore earlier?"

His eyes flicker between Theodore and me. "I said he was as strong as a stallion."

"And?"

His chin drops to his chest. "And he was…dumb as a brick."

"Do you think someone *dumb as a brick* would hold on to a goddamn saw while they're falling off a twenty-foot-tree just so they won't hurt anybody?"

"No, Majesty. I don't think so."

"Me neither." I glare at him. "Please apologize."

"I'm very sorry, Your—"

"Not to me."

The man's face turns whiter than his hair. He pivots a little and faces the boy. "I'm sorry, Theodore."

"Do you accept his apology?" I ask the boy.

"Yes, Majesty. Of course," Theodore replies without hesitation.

"That's very kind of you. I know I wouldn't." I glance back at the chief. "You should thank him."

"Thank you, Theodore. You are very kind.

I apologize again," he mumbles, looking as if he's going to faint.

I wave a dismissive hand. "Leave us. All of you."

My guards escort the chief landscaper outside and secure the doors. Finally, I'm alone with this gorgeous young man.

He holds my gaze with intensity that tears at me. Then he succumbs to my feet and kisses them. "No one has shown me this kind of gentleness before in my life. Allow me to offer myself as Your Majesty's servant forever."

"I've only done you justice, Theodore."

"Please, Majesty, don't refuse me."

"I'm not a fan of servants. As you can see, I'm not one of those rulers who walks around with an army of entourage. If they'd let me, I'd dress myself and cook my own meals. As for Sir Edward and Sir Quinlan, I travel with them only to satisfy their need to serve and obey, not because I fancy their security measures. I'm more than capable of protecting myself, in my own house, at least."

His glistening, arctic eyes lift to me. "Your Majesty can cook?"

I chortle. "I'm an excellent chef. Perhaps I should mentor you instead of Kitchen Master."

He gives a shy smile and rises on one knee. "Majesty, if I may ask, is there really a new faction?"

"I understand your concerns. But with more training, you might not need one after all."

"Seems highly unlikely, Majesty."

"I'm going to be very honest with you, young man. The idea of the new faction is planned in full in my head. Making it happen, on the other hand, is a difficult matter. It's…controversial and has to remain concealed, except from the very few I'll trust to assemble it." I stand. "And become part of it."

"Majesty, I'll do anything to earn your trust." He follows me as I amble down the gravel path in the middle of the solarium that leads to the doors.

"I don't doubt that." My heel suddenly twists over a pebble, and I lose my balance.

"Majesty!" His firm grip constricts my fall. I feel his heated breaths on my face, his strong arms around my waist. My hands, involuntarily, squeeze his biceps.

God, help me.

My palms slide to his chest. Goosebumps roll across my skin as we make eye contact. His eyes fasten on me, on my lips, breath and pulse racing against one another. My gaze roves over his features with equal hunger.

From the moment I laid eyes on Theodore, I've fantasized about breaking all the rules with him.

What would he feel like when his body strains against mine? Would he even know what to do? How to penetrate me? If he does, would it be deep or shallow? Rough or gentle?

Would he please me?

I've wanted to lie naked with him. But now, I want to experience again the closeness found in an intimate embrace with a man who can look at me like this.

The warmth I've been denied since my husband passed away. The warmth I've denied myself by vowing never to marry again.

My chest moves up and down, and he stares. His cheeks turn red. His manhood prods my stomach even through the thick fabric of my gown and his pants. Heat bridges our bodies: his desire, *my* desire.

"Thank you, Theo. May I call you that?"

"Your Majesty may call me anything you wish." He gulps, dragging his eyes to mine.

"I shall hold you to this." I smirk. "You may release me now."

His lips shiver as he withdraws his arms.

"Of course."

I glance down, sizing up his erection. He's ready for me. Completely accessible if I command him to take off his pants.

But I shall not.

Not now.

"You're a lot naughtier than I thought."

He follows the path my eyes have taken, and his jaw drops, his cheeks a burning crimson. His hands quickly fall over the front of his pants. "I…I," he mumbles, out of breath, his eyes shut.

"Don't panic. It's quite normal that you feel this way."

"No, it's not. No matter how sensational Your Majesty is, I mustn't… I'm so ashamed."

"You shouldn't be. It's an involuntary reaction. Honest. And I like honesty."

"Your Majesty is very generous with your mercy, but still, I've sinned." He swallows. "I'm ready for any sort of chastisement."

"As in…punishment?"

"Yes."

I arch a brow. "Do you like to be punished, Theo?" His build and looks resemble Quinn in many forms. Perhaps they share the same needs as well.

He looks at me in wonder. "I don't think

any man would, Majesty."

"You'd be surprised." I laugh under my breath. "Regardless, I'm not going to punish you. You're neither at the Temple nor are you a priest anymore. Your sins are between you and God. Besides, if I start punishing every man who has an erection when he stands this close to me, I'll run out of time."

He barely smiles, but his posture relaxes.

"Sensational is an interesting word. Not beautiful or attractive, but sensational. Is that how you see me?"

He sighs. "Please forgive my insolence, Majesty. I don't know what demon has possessed me today."

"Spare me the nonsense and answer the question."

His head lowers in defeat. "Yes."

For several moments silence falls between us. No noise but our breathing. No reaction but the swelling, ebbing internal pattern of desire.

Underlying my royal persona, there's a girl whose blood pumps and heart pounds when a boy shows her true infatuation. No matter how hard I try to forget her, the heat in my core is a constant reminder.

"Theodore."

His gaze seeks me out.

"Two weeks from now, expect my visit to discuss the terms and conditions of you joining the new faction."

5.
THEODORE

I reach my room flying off my feet. My heart gallops to escape the confines of my chest. The world feels dreamlike, and the kind of joy I'm experiencing right now scares me.

In two weeks, all my wishes come true.

No one dares call me dumb or mediocre again. I'll no longer be useless or lost. Her Majesty has offered me a place in the world where I can finally belong.

And above all, she's offered me dignity and respect.

Her Majesty…

I close my eyes, and her image invades me. Hair, a blaze of bronze and crimson. Neck, long, white, graceful. Eyes, dangerous, drowning. Lips…

I shake my head, exhaling a long breath. Stinging heat floods my cheeks, my ears and crawls down my throat as our little encounter replays behind my eyelids.

Wake up. She's the Queen. My eyes snap open

in panic, but my…verge…isn't deterred.

"A cold bath is in order."

The water streams and fills the tub as I take off my clothes. My foot touches the water. I hiss but plunge my whole body. What has been hard shrinks to escape the cold.

Not for long.

Even the iciness won't keep the memory from assaulting me again.

It's not every day that I get to have a girl in my arms, let alone a woman of unmatched beauty. A queen. My Queen.

My head tilts back against the cold enamel while I savor the residue of Her Majesty's scent before it washes away. Rose, musk, amber and frankincense. Strong. Sensual.

I stare at my hardness with one thought taking over. Another sin.

You're neither at the Temple nor are you a priest anymore. Your sins are between you and God.

And God is forgiving. It's what I've been taught.

My palm slithers around my shaft, and I close my eyes, my heart thudding against my chest. I replace the memory of me rescuing Her Majesty from a mere fall by one more forbidden. Instead of staring at those luscious red lips, I kiss them. I take them between mine and bite softly. Many times. Then my fingers dive into her hair as my mouth glides down her neck, her collarbone, her...breasts...

A moan escapes me as I remember those ample breasts thrusting against the bodice of her gown, against my chest, falling and rising with every breath.

In my unbridled imagination, I unbutton the dress and let her breasts tumble free upon me. Feel them up. Squeeze. Taste. Suckle.

I rub faster now, my throat too dry to swallow, a warm yet painful pressure gathers in my balls. God, I want her. I want my arms to surround her hips instead of her waist, my hands to roam her generous buttocks, and then take off all her clothes and pull her down on me.

I picture how it feels to be inside a woman, to have my hardness sucked in by a...*pussy*.

My groans become loud. My eyes squeeze shut as I give myself a final rub before a jolt of sweet pain shoots down my spine.

My seed spills hot on my knuckles, the back of my hand and into the water.

Trembling in the aftermath of my climax, I draw in long breaths. "I'm so going to hell."

***

Fifteen masturbations later—one every day for the past two weeks and two today so I can

46

meet Her Majesty without disgracing myself—she honors me with her visit.

I bow. "Good evening, Your Majesty."

Her perfect lips curve with a charming smile as she takes in my chamber. "Good evening to you, Theo. How are you feeling today?"

"Wonderful. I'm very excited. How are you feeling, Your Majesty?"

"I feel great. Thank you for asking." She takes a seat, her two guards standing on either side of her. "I like what you've done with the place." Her eyes take another sweep of the room, lingering on the floral arrangements I've designed to make the room more presentable for her visit. "You seem to have learned something from landscaping after all. Kitchen Master has informed me about your improvement as well. I see that all you needed was less pressure and more motivation."

"Thank you, Majesty. Yes, and if I may, I've made some desserts, too, for Your Majesty to try." I step backwards, laughing nervously, until I reach a granite console where I've laid a basket of fresh pastries of my making. My hands shake when I grab it along with a plate and fork. I move to her side, put everything on the table next to her and return to my place before her.

She eyes the basket for a few seconds before her gaze shifts toward me, her expression impossible to read. The guards fix me with a death glare.

What have I done?

I've spent all day gathering Bavarian roses, tulips, sunflowers and crimson cloaks that match her hair, baking cinnamon bread and cherry macaroons because Kitchen Master has informed me they're her favorite. All to impress her. To show her that I can learn, that I'm worthy of her trust. Have I offended her instead? I feel all the blood rush out of my face.

"Majesty, if I... I was just..." I stammer.

She looks at the basket again, but this time she grabs a piece of cinnamon bread and takes a bite.

My heart skips a beat.

"Not bad at all." A small smile tugs the corners of her lips.

"Thank you, Majesty." I breathe again.

"Walk with me." She rises and marches to the door. "Oh, and bring the basket."

***

I take a silent trip with Her Majesty and her escorts across the palace and to a three-story house on the Royal land located a few acres behind her quarters.

48

I doubt anyone resides inside. Despite the few guards at the doors and the excellent condition of the house, everything about it screams forsaken.

She halts and tilts her chin up. "The lights in this building haven't been turned on since my husband died, but thanks to you, Theodore, it's bright again."

I stare at her for a second, confused. "I'm not sure I follow, Your Majesty. What is this place? And what did I have to do with its revival?"

"This used to be the dwelling of the Royal theatre performers," she says. "Every week, brilliant shows were created exclusively for our pleasure. To entertain my husband, my son and myself. I used to love it so much, but when I became a widow I was too sad to enjoy any merry endeavor, so I set them free to entertain the rest of the world instead."

At the Temple, they've taught us so much about the Royal history, but little is mentioned about the late king. As far as I know, they were only married for three years before he was killed in battle. Their union resulted in the birth of Prince Timothy. He's seventeen now and engaged to a foreign Princess with whom he lives until his coronation next year as the King of her country.

A nice addition to Her Majesty's realm.

But my teachings speak of nothing about how the Royals entertain themselves.

"So this is the new faction? Royal theatre?" I ask, more perplexed than ever. I've never been engaged in any artistic work my whole life. Nor do I possess any trade qualities. What could Her Majesty possibly see in me to give me a post here?

"Accompany me inside. I shall explain everything." She climbs the steps to the entrance.

I follow without a word. Sir Quinlan and Sir Edward attempt to enter with us, but she orders them to remain outside. I can't help but noticing their pinched mouths and narrowed eyes.

***

Inside, the interior is empty, which makes the house even bigger than I think. Bigger than the Temple itself. The walls have drawings of men and women dancing and feasting, children playing with animals, floral patterns and bright colors. I swirl around, smiling in spite of my confusion, instantly sucked into a merry mood.

She leads the way to a vast room with a stage. An auditorium.

"Is this where they used to perform?" My

voice echoes against the walls.

"Yes." She takes a seat on the front bench. "Come, Theo. Sit beside me."

I wet my lips and take a deep breath, clutching the basket handle, my steps hesitant. Sitting this near to her may trigger my…indiscretion. Especially here. Alone like this. Again.

I set the basket between us and sit, unable to believe how my willpower is reduced to a bakery holder. I sigh, my gaze on the granite floor, my weakness disturbing.

"The people who lived here were self-sufficient," she begins. "They grew their own food, cooked their own meals, made their own clothes, and above all, created art. Very passionate people."

I look up to speak, but I'm dazed, eyes unswaying from her mouth. She takes a macaroon and tastes it. The color of cherry blends with her lips as if they're joining in a kiss.

Perspiration touches my forehead.

"The new faction apprentices are going to be even better," she says. "Self-sufficient so they won't rely on any other faction and remain a secret. Strong to be able to defend themselves. Passionate to entertain me."

I nudge myself to awareness. "I've never

been to a theatre before nor have I seen a performance anywhere. Pardon my ignorance, Majesty, I still don't understand how this will be the place for someone like me."

"The entertainment I seek now is not theatrical."

"Then what kind of entertainment does Your Majesty seek?"

She eyes me from head to toe. "Sex."

I blink, and I blink once more. "Majesty, I...I..."

"Lost for words? Taken aback?" She takes another bite.

"Yes." Appalled even. Yet it seems that all my blood has rushed to my groin.

"Scared, too, perhaps?"

"No," I answer before I think. Perhaps I should be scared. Terrified. We're alone. No one can hear us but the few guards outside. *Her* guards. She may act upon her wish right here right now. How would I stop her? She'd have me killed if I violently resist. All I can do is beg her to spare me or run.

Can I? Would I?

It's hard enough to resist her allure when I haven't tasted it yet. Once I kiss those lips, once I touch that body, I'm doomed. My eyes widen as I swallow a gasp.

"Good. Because I shall never harm you,"

she assures me.

I barely gather my strength to speak again. "Majesty already knows I don't have the necessary experience in the *proposed department.*"

"I can assure you the required skills are easily learned." She smirks.

"But—"

"I understand you've been a Temple boy, but I also know that you are considering my offer." She leans forward, her scent numbing my conscience, setting a pulse jumping through my manhood. "Your mind might be refusing the whole principle, but your body is betraying you. Your desire for me, young man, is evident."

I don't even attempt to hide my crotch.

"I don't think it's an involuntary reaction anymore," she says. "You fantasize about me now, don't you? Perhaps you've even acted based on those fantasies in the privacy of your bedroom?"

Her gaze doesn't falter. It sees right through me. I nod in sweet surrender.

"I want you, too, Theo." She arches a delicate eyebrow, her gaze studying my features. "So much."

Her voice, her declaration, melt through my senses. "Not more than I do." I speak without thinking again. My jaw falls as my words register in my head. "Dear God. I can't believe I've said that out loud."

She bites her lower lip, and the last of my willpower shatters. If she tells me to take of my clothes now, I will. Gladly.

Please say the words.

But she leans back. "Listen carefully. This is not a commitment to be taken lightly. The offer comes with multiple privileges—riches and esteemed status—but also very harsh terms."

"I'd like to listen to those terms," I say eagerly.

"You'll reside here at all times. Traveling outside the Royal land without permission or security is not allowed. For my safety and yours, no one will ever know about the reality of this faction, not even my escorts. You are never to speak of the nature of your duties, except to the other members."

"Other members?"

"Yes. This arrangement is only exclusive on your side; you'll never be with another person again, which means you'll never marry or have children of your own."

"These are very harsh terms indeed." Lightheaded, I rub a brow. The scrambling thoughts in my head are hard to understand.

No man in his right mind would say yes to those terms. Not without a huge compensation. Assurances. More clarifications, at least.

The only clarification I need to hear is when I can be inside her.

"You might think you're obligated to comply, but you're not. I don't expect you to approve or disapprove now," she adds.

I gulp. "Does that mean I still have the right to choose a different faction?"

"Absolutely. You have six weeks left on your trial period. I think it's enough time to make up your mind."

"Of course."

"As much as I want you, Theo, I will never have you without your full consent."

I wish I had no choice so I can blame it all on her power, my helplessness, fate...anything. Anything but my own desire. My own weakness. My own demons.

If I say yes, I have no excuses.

Yes.

"You're a bastard, aren't you?" Her question snatches me from my daydream.

I grimace. "Yes, Majesty. I haven't met my family."

"You didn't join the Temple willingly. They took you in as their duty. Which means you didn't run away from a commitment, you simply didn't make one in the first place."

"Yes."

"But now you will. You are going to choose, with your own will, which faction you shall belong to for the rest of your life. Do you understand?"

"Yes, Majesty. It's like taking a vow."

"It's exactly a vow." She tosses me a dark look of warning. "Breaking one is a serious crime in my book. For me, it's treason. Are you aware of what I do to traitors?"

"They're tortured to death...with no chance for mercy."

She nods. "Now you know what's at stake whether you commit to my faction or another. Do you have any questions?"

"I do."

"I'm listening."

Insolently, I let my eyes travel down her body, envisioning the time I'd explore it while it's naked. "The nature of my...duties, is it normal? Like any man and woman? Or are there some...abnormalities?"

"It's normal for the most part, but I do have my kinks."

"Kinks?" I shake my head. "Are they dangerous or...painful?"

"Only if you want them to be."

My breaths come out rapid but shallow. "Do I get to refuse to engage in some of those activities if—"

Her index finger hushes my lips. "I said I'd never have you without your full consent. This applies every time and in every way."

A tingling spreads down my spine, and I moan. The feeling of her skin on my mouth is just too much. Reflexively, I kiss it.

She takes her hand back. My heart flutters as I drag my gaze back to hers. "But I'm the only one who is allowed to act upon her urges," she warns me again. "You follow. Never lead."

"I understand. I'm sorry."

"It's all right. I'll let this one go." Another piece of the macaroon finds her mouth. I picture her nibbling something else entirely.

Never in my eighteen years have I ever imagined myself to succumb to temptation like this. All teachings, all principals gone in a few weeks. She must have me under a spell.

"Do you want the rest of it?" She holds what remains of the macaroon before me.

Do I want it? To savor what her lips have touched? To lick where her taste has lingered?

"Of course."

She gives me another one of her triumphant smirks, her fingers approaching my mouth again.

A test.

I take the macaroon with my teeth, careful not to touch her fingers. If I do, I won't be able to help myself. I've already failed the test of God. I don't wish to fail hers too.

"Good boy," she says.

6.
HER MAJESTY

On my way out, I lick my fingers one by one. Liquid desire pools between my legs. That boy has got me hot and bothered with that shameless look over my body and the big twitches of his cock.

Thoughts of ripping his pants and riding him, taking it all inside, have tickled me, but that would ruin all the fun. His full consent isn't enough. His full surrender is required, too. He still needs training to understand how to please a woman like me.

Theodore is a virgin. My virgin. Everything he is, everything he learns will be for me.

I've never before fantasized about teaching a man how to touch me for my own gratification. I do now. It's seductive. A promise of far, far more than a quick, anonymous coupling.

"Where is the boy?" Quinn asks.

"Inside. He can find his way back." Darkness accompanies us as we march. "Tell Sir Connor to bring some men tonight."

He sighs painfully. "Yes, Majesty."

"I want them all like you." I smirk. "Strong enough to take a beating."

"As you wish."

"Oh, where are my manners? Tell him to bring a couple of women, too. I know how fucking hard you both get after watching."

***

The men—or the bulls—Sir Connor has brought line up in my playroom, fully dressed and blindfolded, each holding a leather bag.

A bag of toys, I presume.

I pick three of them and dismiss the rest. When I order them to strip, the guards and my escorts tense, fully alert. The men are really big.

Sometimes, I don't understand why people with such strength find pleasure in pain and humiliation.

Who am I to judge? A woman who inflicts pain, to the soul before the flesh, for her own joy and release.

I take off my robe and touch them, feeling their hard muscles against my hands and naked body. Not aroused, though. Bulging muscles rarely turn me on. "Do you belong to someone else?"

"Not permanently," the bald one says. The

other two, one black and one blond, shake their heads.

"If I open these bags, I won't find collars?"

"Only a new one," the bald man replies, and the blond says the same.

"And you, boy?" I ask the one that remains.

"I apologize, but I don't like collars, Majesty."

"No apology needed." I study his body, his cock. How is this man still single? I hope he's not lying to me. I hate to see him hanged. I'd love to play with that fine piece of ass again after tonight.

With a firm grip on his shoulders, I push him to his knees. "Is there anything else I need to know?" My lips are beside his ear.

"No, Majesty."

I straighten my back. "Well, I must warn you, boys. You are mine for tonight, and I'm not in the mood for safewords. You know what this means?"

"It's an honor to be yours, Your Majesty. Tonight and every night," the blond says.

The other two remain silent except for the assenting grunts that escape their mouths. Obviously, they're more experienced than the blond and know they have one hell of a night ahead of them.

"Now is your only chance to leave, boys. If you have a change of heart, the door is open. You'll be escorted home safely. No questions asked. No consequences."

I wait for a minute, but the boys don't move.

"Fine." I gesture for Ed and Quinn to search the boys and empty their bags. When they're done with the black one, I play with him a little until they finish with the rest.

"Do you have a pet name?" I ask, picking a riding crop from the toys emptied from his bag in front of him.

"Malek, Your Majesty."

"Malek? That's Arabic for king."

"Yes, Majesty."

"Oh, boy, you are bad. Do you really think I, Queen Elysia, will call you king?" I crop him on the back.

He barely flinches. "I don't think so."

My cropping continues on the same spot three times. Each hit harder than the last. He jumps. "I don't think so, what?"

"I don't think so, Majesty."

"You like to misbehave on purpose, don't you?" I eye the silver cuffs in his pile of toys. "Cuff yourself and get on all fours. Tonight, you're my bitch." I hit him again.

"They're all yours, Majesty," Ed announces.

I glance at the other two piles and the men waiting for their turn. Floggers, canes, crops, cuffs and shackles. The collars are new as they said. The bald man has some rope. The blond has butt plugs. Interesting.

"On your knees, boys. My escorts will collar you now."

Ed and Quinn place the collars on the boys' necks and take their places near my favorite bench. The kneeling bench.

I grab the leashes and hook them to the collars. "Come on, boys." I drag them to the bench. They don't resist as their knees scrape the floor.

I hold their arms up one by one and put some leather wrist cuffs on them. Then I shackle their ankles. They lay face-down over the bench, and I clip their wrist cuffs to the eyehooks on it.

Warm shivers engulf me as I take in the scene.

Excitement.

Need.

And I haven't laid a hand on them yet.

My fingers tighten in the blond's hair, fisting it, possessing him. I feel my pussy clench in a familiar way as I pull his head up with a sharp intake of breath from him. "You're giving yourself to me tonight, boy?"

"Yes, Majesty."

I glance at his cock. "Oh, you are eager to give yourself to me tonight, aren't you?"

"Yes, Majesty. Please."

"Do you trust me?"

"With my life, Majesty."

I release his hair and trace light, lazy patterns across his left ass cheek, then his right. "I'm going to turn that pretty, pale ass red now, boy."

He quivers with anticipation.

I use my hand first. A few spanks and swats, enough to sting. Then I bite each cheek hard enough to draw a couple gasps of pain from him. I rub the marks with my hands. "That looks beautiful." I sit on the floor behind him and alternate biting him with stroking his cock, until he squirms from the need and pleasant pain flowing through him and begs for release.

I stand and get his flogger, oil can and one of the butt plugs. "You cannot come. It's way too early." I lay the props on the floor except for the flogger. I whip him once on each cheek. He flinches.

I drop the tool and use the oil on his asshole.

"Oh God," he says, knowing what is to come.

"Oh, yes." I chortle, pressing the plug against his rim. "Push."

He struggles to accept it at first. I monitor his aching muscles and strained face, enjoying every drop of sweat from him and every drop of arousal from my pussy.

He cries out as I seat the plug all the way inside him. Then I leave him tangled with need.

Moving to the bald one, I check out if he has an erection already.

No.

I know what he needs. "Sir Quinlan, tie this one up. I want him wrapped in rope." I unhook the cuffs and bend the bald man's arms behind him. While Quinn binds the back and legs, I tie the wrists. "Make sure you get a piece between his ass cheeks. The pinch will burn with every move."

The man closes his eyes in submission.

Quinn doesn't look at me and works without a word. Time to tease him a little.

"Did you hear me, Sir Quinlan?" I give him a look that says, behave or you'll be next.

"Yes, Majesty," he mumbles. "I'm very sorry."

When he finishes, I point at one pair of spiked heels I keep in the playroom.

He grimaces but obeys and brings them to

me. I order him to put them on my feet.

Again, he obeys, his eyes dark with humiliation.

This turns me on more than anything else. I yearn to play with Quinn and fuck him all night.

Every night.

But for now, I take what I can have.

I turn to the bald man and grab him by the collar. The veins in his neck throb. "Is it too tight?"

"Yes, Majesty," he chokes.

"Good." I leave his collar and squat, resting my weight on the heels, my hands clasping the rope around him. "Can you reach my pussy?"

His beefy fingers find my opening easily. "Yes, Majesty," he slurs.

"Are you willing to let me take anything from you I wish to have while you are bent over this bench and under my control?"

"Yes, Majesty."

"Don't agree if you aren't prepared. I will not stop until I feel the need to stop. This is your only chance to decline."

"I'm yours for tonight, Majesty. To play with me any way you want."

I pull the rope tightly. "Rub my clit." He finally groans.

My head tilts to my escorts. Ed is

composed as always. Quinn is going to burst as always.

The beefy fingers flutter in my pussy as I grab and release the rope. "Don't hold back, Majesty, please," he gasps. "Please."

I grip his collar again. "I won't."

His fingers move with eagerness. His cock is jutting from a tangle of pubic hair. His face is wet with sweat and tears and yet desperate for release.

"Don't come. I haven't given you permission yet. Stop touching me."

"Yes, Majesty," he utters painfully, removing his fingers.

I stand and walk to the black boy. I shove him in the ass with my spiked heels. "Move, bitch."

"Yes, my Queen." He crawls on his forearms and knees to the bench. I kick him with every pace and grab a butt plug on the way.

Slowly, I push it in his asshole.

"No, Majesty. It's too rough."

"Shut the fuck up. You're a big boy. You can take it."

He whines, beyond coherent speech.

I rub his cock and push the plug again. It slides easier now. "See? You only needed me to play with your cock, right?"

He doesn't answer.

My palm smacks his ass. Not gently, but a hard, stinging smack that makes him cry out. "Answer me, bitch. You needed me to play with your cock, didn't you?"

"Yes!"

"Yes, what?" I bite him.

"Yes, Majesty!"

"Very good. Take it all bitch." The plug disappears inside him.

I take one of the bald man's canes and pick the blond's flogger from the floor. Then I stab my heel in the back of bitch, forcing him down on his stomach. The other heel finds his back, too, as I balance my pose, standing on top of him. "Does it hurt, bitch?"

"Yes, Majesty," he sobs.

I almost giggle. "It's going to hurt some more." I use the flogger and the cane on the kneeling men. Right and left. Left and right. Their loud moans throb in my cunt. I give the man under me a couple of lashes, and his squirms almost make me fall. Stepping down, I stomp on his fingertips. Those fingernails will be blue tomorrow.

I drop the tools and lunge at the two tied-up men. Slapping their faces and asses, biting them, scratching their inner thighs with my nails, pinching their nipples until they scream, choking them, and finally holding their balls in my fists.

Their heads jerk around. Their breathing comes out shallow.

I squeeze gently, and they rattle as if they're going to die. I crack a laugh, on the edge of release, as I do it again and again. Bring them from death and back. Then I stop and rest against the bench.

With my heel, I nudge bitch in the forehead. "Get up." He lifts his head, and I push him into my pussy. "Get busy."

He flicks his tongue over my clit, making me jump but not getting me off. My fists grab the blond by his hair and the bald by his collar and push them onto my tits.

"You did well, boys. You can all come after me."

I tilt my head back, imagining the three boys to be Quinn, Ed and Theo, and wait for my sweet release.

***

It's my turn to watch.

Two whores in nothing but blindfolds. Ed and Quinn nude. Me, still naked. The room just for us.

"Go ahead, boys. Please these ladies like you should please the woman you love. Please yourselves like you *are* with the woman you love."

Ed and Quinn stare at each other in agony, and then they both flip the whores on their stomachs and take them from behind.

Their gazes are on me.

Their minds are with me.

Their exerted thrusts are for me.

Their tears are because of me.

I touch myself and come again.

7.

THEODORE

In the past six weeks, I've baked hundreds of pastries, cooked meals, planted crops, made clothes, trained with the Royal Guards, made a home out of the forsaken house, and most importantly, built the bridge that connects it to Her Majesty's quarters.

'Easy access' she has called it. I can't agree more.

Building that bridge is the most pleasant task I've ever had. The path that will lead me to a more pleasant job. To her. To be a man for her. With her.

Forever.

And forever can start today.

When I give Her Majesty my final decision.

My future.

Myself.

The physician knocks on my door. I let him in for my weekly inspection. Since my first visit of the house, Her Majesty has sent me the best healthcare workers to check and maintain my health. Also, to ensure I'm disease-free so I can…pledge myself to her.

If I choose so.

Today.

***

I wait for the Queen in the house as she has commanded. I stand on the stage. Sweat wets my hands and the back of my neck. When she arrives, my heart thuds against my chest.

She's elegant as always. Her hair, a blazing waterfall against her skin, cascades down to her waist. Her dress, golden and green, is beautiful, yet less complicated than usual. *Easy access?*

A smile trembles on my mouth.

She smiles back.

Then she takes a seat, her escorts guarding her. "Are you ready, Theo?"

I bow. "Yes, Majesty."

"Let's hear it. What is your choice? Which faction would you commit yourself to for the rest of your life?"

"I choose…" I take a breath, my heart pounding in my temples. This is it; the moment I've been waiting for; the moment I've been afraid of.

If I say what I desire, I give up my rights for love, family and virtue. There's no turning back. I can be a priest, a cook, a builder, a fighter, a gardener, anything, but my body has chosen for me. Everything in me is screaming, begging for one thing only.

Her Majesty.

My doom. My hell.

"Yes, Theo, what do you choose?"

My gaze unwarily seeks hers out, and all doubts and regrets disappear. "I choose to pledge myself to Her Majesty's Art House."

I let out my breath.

"Excellent choice." She smiles again. "Sir Quinlan, Sir Edward, do you witness?"

"Yes, Majesty," they say in unison.

"Then please report the news to High Priest." She looks up at them. "Once you do, return to secure the bridge and wait there to escort me back to my chambers. I have important things to discuss with Theodore."

8.
HER MAJESTY

When Theodore and I are alone, I tell him to take me to his bedroom.

"Are you nervous?" I ask as we step inside.

"I am," he answers, his heartbeats louder than the door when he shuts it.

"Relax. I'm going to be very gentle." My fingertips caress his face. Then I feel his arms until my hands fit in his wet palms. Our fingers intertwine, and I pull him gently to the bed.

He complies, as if in trance, his eyes never leaving mine, his body burning with need.

"I want to look at you. Take off your clothes," I demand. His fingers work the buttons of his coat fast. "Wait. Take it slow with the shirt. Your first lesson: fast is never good in bed."

He chuckles. "Yes, Majesty."

He takes his time, and I trace the contours of his chest and abdomen, my nipples hardening. As he finishes, I slide my hands underneath, exploring the firm flesh, exposing his upper body.

He sucks in successive breaths, his muscles clenching under my touch. Drops of wetness gather between my thighs.

I draw near and kiss his neck, then my tongue glides up to his earlobe. "You're very sexy." My hand undoes his belt and goes inside his pants. His head falls on my shoulder, his gasps hot on my skin as I feel his long, engorged cock. I moan. My pussy throbs. "It's a big one you have." I rub him, and he quivers.

I get my hand out of his pants and pull away. "If this is too much for you, I can wait."

He shakes his head. "Please don't. I have been waiting for this moment for weeks, Majesty."

I, too, have been waiting for this moment.

For years.

Fifteen to be exact. Since my king. The only man I've allowed to fuck me—with his cock anyway.

"Then take off your pants," I demand.

Theodore rises and strips before me. His dick blatantly stands out from his body, long, thick, hard. I don't have to glance down to know my nipples are equally hard. I don't have to glance up to know he's staring at them.

"Now what do I do?" I hear the roughness of lust in his voice.

"Come closer."

He steps forward until his toes hit mine, his cock at my mouth level. I fight the temptation to lock my lips around him—something my pride has never allowed me to experience. However, if I do, he'll come in my mouth in a second. "Now take off *my* clothes."

His vibrant eyes gleam.

"This gown is very easy to take off," I say. "I wore it especially for you."

With shaky fingers, he works the first button, his fingertips caressing my chest. "I know. For easy access."

I chortle. "Yes. Beware, though. I'm completely naked underneath."

The next button pops fast.

And the next.

Until I sit naked on his bed.

I note his rapid and scorching breaths, the heat in his cheeks, and the clear liquid spilling from his cock.

And above all, the hunger in his gaze.

"Yes, Theo. Look at me. I want to see in your beautiful eyes how much you desire me. How twisted with need you are for me."

"Please let me touch you. I'll do anything,"

he barely whispers.

"I know you will." I take his hands and put them on my breasts.

He groans. The circles of his palms start slow, soft, but then they grow into greedy squeezes. "Am I doing this right?"

"Yes. You're a natural." I tilt my head back, moaning with pleasure. "How hard my nipples are tells you how well you're doing your job."

He feels them with his thumbs. "They're really hard."

"Yes, they are. Do you like my tits, Theo? Look at me when you answer."

He lifts his head, his hands pressing harder. "Your Majesty's... They're so beautiful."

"My Majesty's what?"

His lips and dick twitch. "Your Majesty's breasts."

I shake my head teasingly.

He bites his lip. "Your Majesty's *tits* are so beautiful."

"Suck them."

I watch as he wets his mouth and the distance between it and my painfully engorged nipples shrinks. Then I feel a hot, wet tongue tentatively rasp my flesh, there on the very tip of my tit.

Once. Twice. Thrice. Left tit. Right tit. He

licks me, like a hungry dog. Top side of my nipple, underside, the very tip again.

"Like this?" His voice shakes.

My fingers tangle in his thick hair, pulling him down. My other hand grabs his tight ass. "Yes."

His licks turn into long mouthful suckles. My cunt clenches; hot liquid dribbles down my thigh. "Do you know how else to be sure you're doing a good job?"

His lips release my nipple with a pop. "How?"

"By how wet I become."

"Where?" he asks with hazy eyes.

"My pussy."

His lips part, and his gaze drops to my sex. "Is Your Majesty wet?"

I spread my legs in brazen invitation, a woman shamelessly opening herself to a man. "Discover for yourself."

He goes on his knees, his palms gliding from my tits to my abdomen and onto my cunt. He cups me, shapes me, weighs me. Then he parts me, tunneling through my slick lips until he touches the very tip of me with the very tip of his finger. He gasps. "Your Majesty is…" He stares into me. "Your Majesty's pussy is drenched."

"Yes."

"Would Your Majesty like me to suck it?"

"No." The throbbing in my core is unbearable. "I'd like you to fuck it."

He grunts and clenches his teeth as if in pain.

"Do you want to fuck my pussy?"

"Yes! I want to fuck Your Majesty's pussy so hard." His finger, reflexively, presses my clit.

"Get up."

When he does, I wrap my fist around his erection.

His brows hitch. "Majesty, I will come like this."

"I know." I rub him fast.

"But—"

"If you fuck me now, you won't last for two thrusts. Just come in my hands, then I'll let you inside me."

He exhales a sharp breath. I take his hand and place it on my left tit. He squeezes and groans. His cum spurts in my hands. Once. Twice. Six fucking times. I look at him as his ragged breaths sear my face and sweat covers his forehead.

Our gazes lock for a few seconds before he grabs his shirt and wipes my hand. "I'm sorry about the mess."

I lift my hand to my nose and smell it.

Then I lick my thumb. "I don't mind."

"Oh God."

I glance down, and I see his cock is ready again. "That didn't take long." I kick my slippers off and push myself back on the bed. Once I settle, I part my legs and bend my knees. He stabs his teeth into his lip as he takes a clearer look at my pussy.

"The pocket of my dress," I instruct.

He finds the gown, inserts his hand in the pocket and brings out a small, silver case.

"Open it and take what's inside."

He opens the case and takes out a condom, looking at it unsurprised.

"Do you know what this is?"

"Yes, Majesty. A prophylactic."

I arch a brow. "Have you used one before?"

"No. But I've borrowed one from a friend once."

My eyes narrow with suspicion. "Why?"

He pinches the bridge of his nose, his eyes closed. "There was this girl at the Temple… It's so much easier on Dispensation if you have a girl. I…" He lets out a heavy sigh.

"Did you touch her?"

"Yes."

"How?"

"I kissed her and touched her breasts." He

shakes his head. "That's it."

"That's it?"

"I swear on Your Majesty's life."

"Why didn't you go through with it?"

"I didn't feel anything for her. I couldn't just use an innocent person for my own gain." He glances back at me. "Does Your Majesty despise me now?"

I can't hold my laughter. "Oh, come here, Theo." His eyes light again. He gets on top of me, his knees beside my thighs, his hand holding the rubber. I curve my hands around him in an embrace, cradling his head. "*You're* so innocent. My young virgin," I muse. "I'm about to suck that innocence of yours between the folds of my slick, wet pussy. You're the one who should despise me."

He blinks. "What I feel is the complete opposite of despise."

"I know." I give him a few strokes and place the condom on his hardness. "Rub my cunt before you enter me."

He gently defines the hardened kernel of flesh—my clit—measuring its size, outlining its shape.

I hold his cock and guide it to my opening. "I want you to look at me all the time."

He nods.

"Go ahead."

He pushes himself forward. I moan.

"OH DEAR GOD." He trembles. Hard. "Is… Is Your Majesty all right? Am I hurting you?"

"No. You want me to moan. To scream. The louder the better."

"Okay." He nods again. "Do I do the same move again?"

"Yes. Do as many as you can."

He pulls back out, and rams into me. Again. And again. And again.

He quivers with every thrust, and I cry out as he fills me. "You feel so fucking good, Theodore. So fucking good." I grab his hard ass and push him deeper inside me. "Tell me what you're doing to me."

"I'm fucking Your Majesty. I'm fucking Your Majesty's pussy with my cock." He gasps for breath. "Oh my God. I'm fucking my Queen."

Perspiration drips down my forehead, my nose, plops onto my tits. I don't know who it comes from—me or him. The intensity of his thrusts and his gaze takes my breath away. I haven't been looked at like this in years. I haven't been fucked like this in years.

"Do you feel how my pussy clenches around your cock?" I ask between breaths.

"Yes, Majesty." His strokes are frantic now.

"Do you know what this means?"

"Your Majesty is about to release."

"Yes. Ye-s. Fuck me harder. Make me come."

"Can I come too?"

"Yes!"

My back arches. Our pelvises grind. The sound of our own labored breathing surrounds us.

A cry spreads through my chest and out of my mouth.

Pleasure. Pain.

He buries his face in my hair, nose and lips pressing against my neck as he stifles his growl.

I wrap my arms around his slippery waist and press him to my chest. "I hope your first time was enjoyable."

He straightens his back, wiping his face with the back of his hand. "It was a lot more than enjoyable, Majesty. I shall remember it for the rest of my life."

"The second part is undeniable, but I can assure you nobody's first time is more than enjoyable."

He smiles. "But it was, I swear."

"Well, the next time will be even better."

"As long as there is a next time, I'm happy, Majesty."

I laugh out loud, smacking his ass. "You're trouble, boy. Now get the fuck out of me, please."

He slides out of my center and gets off the bed. I leave the bed as well and reach for my dress. He hurries to grab it. "Your Majesty is going to leave now?"

"Yes."

"May I make Your Majesty some tea? I've baked the cinnamon bread Your Majesty loves."

"No, thank you."

"At least, let me help Your Majesty with your clothes."

I roll my eyes as I stand and turn my back to him. "Fine."

He pushes my hair to the side of my neck to dress me, and then buttons up the gown, fingers lingering on my body. He grabs my slippers, kneels and put them on my feet.

I turn and glance at his rubber-sheathed dick. "You should burn the condom."

"I will, Majesty."

"Have a pleasant day." I start for the door. "And eat well. I need you strong."

He stalks after me. "May I know when I will see Your Majesty again?"

I give him a warning stare. "Whenever I please, Theodore."

"Of course." He shakes his head rapidly. "I meant... I just... I can't wait to see Your Majesty again," he stammers, his glistening eyes beseeching. "Not just for sex."

I study his expression. "Oh God. I hope you're not falling in love with me, young man. That will only break your heart."

9.

THEODORE

I'm not a young man.

Not anymore.

She's made sure of that.

I wait for her every day and every night with only memories of the best day of my life.

The worst.

I remember everything. I've cataloged every inch of her curves, every quiver of her breasts, every gasp of her mouth, every scream. The press of her lips and the lick of her tongue when she kissed my neck. Her first touch on my dick. The hot core of her vulva. The silky-soft hardness of her feminine bud. The soft prickle of her pubic hair grinding into my pelvis while she swallowed me whole.

She's opened a gate that should have remained closed.

Doesn't she know how it feels? To experience such joy once and never again?

It's a hell a lot worse than remaining a virgin; a man who doesn't know what he's missing; a man who only has fantasies of what is the best feeling in the world.

It's not like I can experience it again with someone else.

I'm not allowed.

Even if I am, I don't want to.

I spend another night watching the bridge from the bedroom window, praying for a glimpse of her.

But nothing happens.

I lie in my bed, alone for the seventh night, praying again. This time, for sleep.

At least, when I close my eyes, I see her.

My mind drifts with the darkness. My fingers twirl in long waves of fire. "You have very beautiful hair." My thumb caresses her lips. "And these..." I sigh. "You won't let me kiss them, but in my dream I don't need your permission." My lips part as I approach her face.

"Except that you're not dreaming."

My eyes open lazily, then they snap open. I jump to my feet, my heart fluttering.

She smirks, leaning back against the headboard. "Good morning."

"Good morning to you, Majesty." My voice comes out thick with sleep. I clear my throat, pointing to the bathroom.

She nods. "Don't take too long."

She's here. She's finally here.

I wash the smell of sleep off me but don't put on any proper attire. She's here for one thing, and it doesn't require clothing. I wrap a towel around my waist and return to her.

The lustful look in her eyes satisfies me but doesn't take away the pain of abandonment.

I let the towel drop on the floor.

"I didn't tell you to strip," she says.

"I'm sorry. I thought it was the only thing Your Majesty would ever ask me to do when we're not in bed. I was trying to be a *good boy*."

Her eyes narrow. "What is your problem, Theodore? What do you want? Leave? You know I can't let you do that. More privileges than the ones I grant you? Living on the Royal land in a house that exceeds your dreams, *fucking* your own Queen, isn't enough for you? Or is it more money? I already pay you ten times more than what the Temple used to pay you, but make no mistake, it's for everything you do around this house, not for your body, young man. I'm the Queen. I do not pay for sex. Men literally line up for me to have them, and just for the honor of pleasing me."

My eyes widen in shock. "I've never thought for a second that the more than generous salary Your Majesty pays me was for my body. Your Majesty is a Queen, and I'm not a whore. What we share is a lifetime commitment. An obligation of respect before anything else." The pitch of my voice is higher than I anticipate. I step forward, making sure she sees my face clearly. "And I most certainly do not wish to leave."

"Then what the hell do you want?" she challenges.

"Not your abandonment. Your Majesty must know how much I need you. How much I will always need you. I gave Your Majesty everything. I do not deserve to be punished for it."

Her face darkens. "In that case, I shouldn't have left you this long. I have an obligation toward you, just like you do. I apologize."

I stumble back a step, taken aback. "God forbid I ask Your Majesty to apologize. All I ask for is…the kindness and care Your Majesty has always showed me." I wish for a lot more, though. A kiss. A word of affection. Permission to give her my heart as I've given her my body and soul. But she's made it clear love is another crime in her book.

"I do care about you, Theodore. Your submission is a gift that I honor and respect. I just didn't think you were truly willing to give it yet."

"Willingly, I've pledged myself to Your Majesty. I'm standing before Your Majesty naked. How else can I prove it? Go down on my knees and kiss Your Majesty's feet? Beg Your Majesty to let me serve you? I've done that, too, and I shall do it again if it pleases Your Majesty."

"Much to my surprise, I don't want any of these things from you, Theo. I just want to enjoy myself. Be myself. Elysia, the woman. Not My fucking Majesty."

I sit next to her. "Then let me explore that woman, learn her body, give her pleasure." I open my hands and rest them palms up between us. "Please."

After a few moments or a few hours, she places her hands in mine. It feels as if they clench around my heart instead. Suddenly, I find myself leaning forward, risking everything.

For a kiss.

She leaves my hands and rises to her feet. "Obviously, you seek intimacy, and my kiss is something you treasure to the point of dreaming about it."

I swallow. "It is." It will mean the world to me.

"I'm not going to kiss you, Theo, but I'll give you more today." She unties her cape. It slides over her shoulders and onto the floor. "Do you need to have breakfast first?" Her dress comes off next.

I ogle her. Desire knots inside my stomach. "It's not food that I need to eat."

Kneeling over me, she grasps my dick. "Today, you don't have to wait for my permission or for me to lead."

The thud of my heart shakes my entire body.

"Are you going to shudder like this every time I touch you?" she asks.

"Yes," I answer, still shaking. "It's good shuddering."

She smiles and cups my face with her hands. "And If I told you that today you could go inside me bare, would you shudder some more?"

I stop breathing as I imagine my bare flesh sinking into her bare flesh, and feel my already turgid dick grow longer, thicker. "As much as I love to do that, I don't think I'll be able to pull out in time."

Her eyes dim for a split-second. Then she nibbles my ear. "You don't have to worry about that. I'll use a syringe after."

I don't know what kind of syringe she's talking about, but it's not the time to ask. I push her hair aside and kiss her neck. My arms wrap around her in a tight embrace. Her hair brushes my shoulder and waist softly when she draws back. I keep it secure in my fist behind her back so I can see both her breasts. "Your Majesty is so beautiful."

"Stop calling me that when we're alone," she demands.

I grin. "*You* are so beautiful." I lave her tits with wet swipes of my tongue. Her breaths grow rapid. Mine too.

"You make me so fucking wet. I'll have to ride you now." She has one arm around my back, the other arm sneaking down to my cock. She lifts herself up and guides me to her entrance. Then she pushes her pelvis down.

The weight of her body is more welcome than my next breath.

Wet heat kisses me. Unrelenting pressure. Scalding moisture.

Blood scorches my cheeks and pounds in the temples. I let go of her hair, and it drapes over us. With one hand I grasp her left hip; the other bolsters the small of her back.

She moves up and down, her tits bouncing. I grind my pelvis against hers, and she circles her hips. A chorus of ragged breathing blends with the wet impact of flesh slapping flesh.

My thighs and knees ache. My skin burns with sweat. Pressure radiates inside my groin. My cock twitches. I look into her eyes, fighting back a cry of agony, until I can't anymore.

She stares down at me, face streaked with sweat and sunshine, hair clinging to her cheeks and her breasts.

"Oh, Majesty." I kiss her between the breasts.

"I asked you to stop calling me that."

I caress her cheek with the back of my hand. "Elysia." No name tastes sweeter than hers.

She gives a small smile, but it instantly vanishes. "Did you like this time better?"

I nod. "You were right about that. Would I like the next even more?"

She rolls off me, my own semen dropping on my legs. "Most likely."

"But you didn't enjoy it this time. I'm sorry. Please let me try again...now." I chuckle.

She walks to the towel on the floor, buttocks gently bouncing, hips swaying. "You'll get better with time, and if you don't, there are medications to make you last long enough."

I grimace. She's switched to ruler mode in a fraction of time. "Why are you upset? Did I do something wrong?"

"Not at all." She grabs the towel. "I'll go clean myself."

I run and block her way to the bathroom.

"I'll do it for you, but first tell me what upsets you. Is it the way I touched you? How I looked at you? How I said your name?"

"No, Theo. In fact, I liked all of that. That's why I'm upset."

"Why?"

"Because I'm greedy, and what was supposed to be a one-time reward will become a regular request, which will lead you to believe there's more to this relationship than what it really is."

"I know exactly what this relationship is. Sex. Lust. Sinful pleasure. You don't have to remind me that I can't have feelings for you every time you see me."

She shakes her head. "Oh dear God. It's already happened, hasn't it?"

"Yes, and there's nothing even a powerful queen like you can do about it. Can I give you that bath now?"

10.
HER MAJESTY

Immersed in the water from the waist down, my eyes closed, my head resting on a soft pillow, my hair trailing behind the bathtub edge, I feel Theodore's eyes on my naked body.

The body that tortures more than it pleasures.

The body that enslaves and never sets free.

The body of a monster.

A sadist.

"Do women touch themselves for release like men do?" His words and wet hands on my stomach yank me out of my thoughts.

"Yes. They tell their men to touch them, too." I open my eyes and tilt my head to look at him. "If a man is not good with his hands, he's pretty much useless."

He soaks a washcloth and uses it on my abdomen. "I don't understand. Shouldn't a man please his woman with his penis?"

"Dick is overrated. Rarely does the trick. It's everything else that matters." My orgasms for the past fifteen years prove it. Even before. "I don't fuck you for your dick, Theodore. Any healthy man can fuck. I do it because of the way you look at me. That primal need in your eyes. That innocence." I place my palm on his face. "That surrender."

"I'd like to make you come with my hands."

I laugh under my breath. "No. I have a long list of men who do that for me."

He grinds his teeth, his face strained.

"Surprised?" I ask.

He says nothing.

"Jealous?"

"Do they look at you the same way I do?"

"They don't look at me at all. They're blindfolded when they touch me. The only stares I get are from my guards."

He stares at me incredulously. "They watch you?"

"Watch over me, but they're men. They can't help themselves."

"It must be torture for them."

"It is." On so many levels.

"Thank God I didn't join the Royal Guards."

I laugh.

"Still, I want to make you come." He leans so close I can feel his breath on my face. "I'll look at you the whole time."

"I said no."

"Your nipples are hard at the thought. Your body is betraying you, Elysia." He gazes at me, his fingers already teasing my nether lips.

"You're disobeying me."

One of his fingers finds my clitoris. I press my lips to muffle a gasp.

"You can either break my hand or let me touch that bud inside you that seems to drive you insane." He circles it slowly.

"Or both."

"There's that, too." He prints little kisses on my shoulders, neck and chest, his eyes never leaving mine, his finger finding a good rhythm.

"At least, let's do this right. Drain the tub and get in."

"Yes, my Queen." He removes the stopper. His stare is pinned to my pussy as the water flows away.

"What are you doing?"

"Marveling at the beauty of your sex, pink and wet between a fringe of damp waves." He licks his lips.

I part my legs wider. "You can still marvel at it while your fingers are inside. Get in."

His knees settle next to my legs. I slide

down a little. His finger teases my clit again. His stare, as promised, stays on me. "Do I insert my finger inside you, like I do with my dick?"

"Yes. More than one. But keep touching the clit."

His middle finger slides in. "Clit?"

"The bud."

His index fingers follows. His thumb applies the perfect pressure on my clit. My gasps go loud.

"You're getting wetter."

Of course, I am. I glance at his cock. "You're getting harder."

He bends forward, his kisses searing my body. "Should I go faster?"

"Yes!"

His mouth suckles on my tits as his fingers slide in and out of me. His cock pokes me. Hard as wood.

I cup his ears, staring back at him. "Talk to me."

"Your pussy is clenching around my fingers, crushing them," he says between suckles.

I moan.

"You love foul words as much as you love my wet tongue on your nipples and my thumb on your clit, don't you?"

"Hell yes," I gasp.

A drip of preparatory moisture squeezes out of his cock. He grunts, sharing my pleasure and my pain. I stroke him. The hardness sends more juice down my core.

His mouth leaves my nipples, gasping with me now. "See how hard you make me? I want you so much, Elysia. I want my cock inside your pussy." His eyes blaze with desire.

Raw, animalistic desire.

I stroke him faster, his fingers pumping inside me. A familiar pressure gathers in my belly and moves down. "I want to feel your cum on me." I hold his gaze and welcome the pangs of desire that erupts between my legs.

And the hot cum that sprays my neck, chest, abdomen and the tip of my pussy.

"I love this moment, when you come for me," he says, his voice and face strained. "I'll love it even more if you'll kiss me."

I won't lie. I have considered it. When he's this close to me, when he's just pressed and released every pleasurable nerve in my body, I want to kiss him, too.

"I will not kiss you, Theodore."

His gaze shifts from my eyes to my lips. "Please."

My nipples harden again. "No."

He draws even closer. "I'm begging you."

My pussy throbs again. "I said no."

"Just one kiss. I'm dying, Elysia," he pleas.

I savor his pain, his need, the urgency in his voice, the humiliation on his face as he's less than an inch from my lips and still can't take what he yearns for. "How far will you go to have that kiss?"

"I'll do anything. I'll follow you to hell."

"You've already done that."

"Who knows? I pray for forgiveness every night."

"Let me hear that prayer."

"God, forgive me for I've fucked my Queen, and it felt so fucking good," he says, stressing the last part.

I smile.

"Forgive me for I'm going to do it again, and again until my last breath," he continues. "Forgive me for I follow her now. Forgive me…for I love her."

My smile vanishes. Sweet rage courses through my veins. In a swift move, I squeeze his neck with my grip, choking him. His eyes widen in shock. His face turns crimson. "Don't say that word again," I warn him.

He struggles with his breathing, but he doesn't fight my hand. "I'll say it…as long…as I'm alive."

My nipples harden to the point of pain.

"You fucking prick."

His eyes tear. "Nothing you do or say will change how I feel for you," he rasps.

"Fuck you."

"Gladly."

I release his neck for a second to push him off me and force his back on the edge of the tub. Then I choke his wild breaths again as I straddle him. "Your safeword is Tim. Say it or tap the tub three times if you want me to stop for any reason."

I don't wait for his response.

I fuck him.

I slap him, bite him, dig my nails in his skin, pull his hair, and he gazes at me, painfully, anticipating my finish.

I do.

My cunt ripples around him in the aftermath of one of the strongest orgasms I've ever had.

Fisting, relaxing, fisting, relaxing about his cock, his heart.

Too much, not enough.

I let go of his neck and get out of the tub. I glance at him as he sits naked and wounded like this. Shaking.

He doesn't look back at me.

I open the cabinet under the sink and get a towel. Sitting next to him on the edge of the tub, I cover him with the towel and my embrace. "I'm sorry. I shouldn't have done that now. Should have walked you through it first. Prepare you for my craziness."

"Why didn't you?"

"I was too aroused."

His shadowy eyes glance up at me. "You came fast this time, even though you released a few minutes ago. So this is what you like the most?"

My chest tightens. Yes, I like to watch how obsequious a man can become.

Not once have I felt guilty about it.

Until now.

I wipe his tear-stained face. "Are you in pain?"

"Yes."

"Why didn't you safeword? Obviously, you're not made for this."

"I'm a strong man. I can take what you've done and ten times more...Majesty."

I note the bitterness in his tone as he calls me formally. "You should have stopped me since you don't find pleasure in pain."

"Don't I?"

"Obviously," I repeat.

"Then why do I feel like this?"

"Like what?"

"My body doesn't hurt, but I'm aching on

the inside. You made me feel powerless, humiliated, like a slave, and yet…" A tear drops from his eyes.

"You'd let me hurt you again, just to please me, because you love me." I finish his sentence.

"Yes." He breaks.

Pain comes in different shapes. The marks on the body can heal. The scars fade with time. The pain that's inside, however, is eternal.

Marks you up forever.

Fucks you up forever.

That's what I like the most.

I let him cry on my chest, giving him the aftercare he deserves. "You're not my slave. I don't own slaves."

"I know, and everything you did was by my consent. I only didn't think it'd hurt this much."

"Let me make it up to you. You've been very good to me. You've earned a reward."

He lifts his head off my chest, his stare eager. "One kiss from you."

11.
HER MAJESTY

I roll my eyes. "How about breakfast? Or lunch? Or both?"

"Why are you so afraid to kiss me?" His jaws tense.

"I beg your pardon?"

"Do you fear falling in love with me, too?"

My lashes flutter. "How insolent! I think you secretly liked what I've just done to you because you're basically asking for another punishment."

He gets out of the tub, his chest stained with sweat and faint blood from my scratches, and kneels before me. "You said you wouldn't kiss me because you didn't want me to fall for you. It's clear that I'm way past that, and nothing will ever change how I feel. Why won't you kiss me?"

Because I won't feel the same for you.

That's what I'm afraid of.

"Theodore, I'm tired of this game. This drama. I get that you're young, and this whole life is new to you, but I don't have the time for this. Your feelings aren't something I can control, but your words and behavior will be as I please."

"What does this mean?"

"It means you should have chosen lunch." I rise and point at the tub. "Fix me another bath."

***

After another fucking and a nice bath, I allow Theo to cook for me.

Naked.

I sit at the dining table, watching as he prepares our meals. His hair slick, smoothed to the back. The muscles in his back, legs and ass ripple when he walks.

"This is not how I imagined cooking for you would be like." He sets the table with dishes and silverware.

I laugh.

"And you're enjoying this because it's humiliating?" He lays a basket of bread and a tray full of salmon rolls, fruit and tiny sandwiches on the table.

"Not just that. I enjoy it because you're very sexy naked, and even though I've had you four times this morning, I'm famished for you."

He chuckles as he turns off the burner under the soup. Then he serves me a dish.

Himself as well. "You're insatiable."

"True."

He smiles. "You should eat, though." He grabs his spoon, takes some of my soup and tastes it. "It's good. Not poisoned or anything."

I laugh again, enjoying the close look at his ass before he takes his seat.

"Why won't you marry?" he asks.

I take a soft roll from the basket. "I've taken a vow."

"But why?"

The same reason I am not worried about you coming inside me.

The secret that once known I'll no longer be the powerful, seductive Queen Elysia that brings men and their kingdoms to the ground.

The truth that I escape.

The worst night of my life.

The night the king died, I didn't only lose him. I lost my second son, too, in childbirth, and the ability to have another. In one hour, Timothy has become a fatherless, only child, and I've become a barren widow.

"A woman with such passion, such beauty, why torture yourself like that?" He sips his soup.

"Trust me, I'm not the one who is tortured." Not by the absence of marriage anyway. This part is fun. Why limit myself to one man when I can have as many as I wish?

"You do what you've done to me today to all the other men who…pleasure you?"

"Only the ones who enjoy it as much as I do."

"Which part do you enjoy the most? Playing with all the men or torturing them?"

"Both."

His bright eyes penetrate me. "You're a sadist."

I ding him with a look that says, I'm done playing games. "I am."

He sighs and breaks a loaf of bread, his brows furrowed.

"I won't do it again with you, if that's what you're worried about."

"But it's part of who you are. You said you wanted to be yourself here, with me." His palm rests on top of my hand. "I want that, too."

"It's a part you don't have to accept, Theo. Our agreement is clear."

"It's a part I have to accept because I love you, Elysia. All of you."

"Young man, are you provoking me on purpose?"

He smiles and sips more soup. "You haven't touched your food."

I take a bite of the soft roll.

"Have you ever fallen in love?" he asks.

I tilt my head back, glancing at the ceiling. "Yes."

"Other than the king?"

"Yes."

"Why aren't you with him?"

I glance back at him. "He refused me."

"What?" He stares at me as if I were mad.

"Not all men surrender to temptation, Theodore."

"Perhaps, but all men surrender to Elysia." I smirk.

"What could be so urgent and dire that made a man refuse your love?"

"Duty."

He shakes his head. "I don't buy it. When was the last time you saw him?"

"I see him every fucking day."

The silver in his hand falls and clinks on the table. "I'm so stupid." His palm leaves my hand and joins his other palm in a tight clasp. "I thought you wouldn't kiss me so you wouldn't feel something for a commoner. A bastard like me. It turns out you won't because you're in love with someone else."

"That's not the reason. I kiss the other men who pleasure me, but I won't kiss *you*."

His hands ball into fists. "So you can

torture me? So you can orgasm watching me suffer?"

"So I won't hurt you," I yell. "I won't be able to feel your kiss the way you want me to. I won't be able to reciprocate a fraction of the affection you show me. It's going to hurt you, and it's going to hurt me." I close my eyes in regret. "I don't wish to hurt you, not like this, Theodore, and I'd rather delude myself that I might with time one day fall for you, or anyone for that matters, than put that false hope to test right now and destroy it for good."

He bows his head in defeat.

"I wish to God I could love you, Theo. At least, I can have you whenever I wish. But my heart belongs to the only man who refused me. The man I torment every day and shall continue to torment for the rest of his life."

The only man who torments me.

I rise from my seat, intending to leave, but he holds my hand.

His glistening eyes lift to me. "I'm sorry. Please stay."

12.
QUINN

"The boy reminds me a lot of myself when I was his age," I start, escorting the Queen back to her quarters.

"Does he?" she mutters.

"Your Majesty doesn't see the resemblance?"

"Not really."

A lie.

To anger me. To stir the doubts that are already killing me.

To make me misbehave.

I fall right into the trap.

"If Your Majesty is going to spend this much time with the boy, we should have him gelded."

She halts, and her head whips toward me, her big eyes bigger. "Have you gone mad?"

Yes.

"Having a faction for just one person, who presumably has artistic merit no one has witnessed, and spending *hours* in his company, alone, are going to start rumors, Majesty."

She raises one eyebrow. "With that logic, I should have you and Edward gelded. I spend more hours with you two than I spend with anyone else…and you see me naked."

I glare at her. I knew she'd find a way to turn the situation on me. My plans always backfire when I'm blinded by jealousy.

She continues down the bridge. "There are going to be others. The Art House is not solely about art anymore. And what I do with my time is completely up to me to decide, Sir Quinlan."

"Please don't call me that."

"I'll call you whatever I wish to call you." She steps in front of me and marches. A gesture that means she doesn't want me to walk by her side or talk anymore.

I stifle all my anger, resentment and jealousy and follow her.

Anywhere. To hell and beyond. It's what I do.

I follow her.

***

When we reach her chamber, she barely greets Edward and enters alone, ordering us to stay guard outside and not to interrupt her for any reason.

Hours pass. She doesn't leave her room

except for dinner.

I wait for her retaliation all night to no avail.

She's ignoring me.

On purpose.

The worst punishment ever.

The next day, she doesn't even look at me while she murmurs a flat 'good morning'.

And the next day.

And the next.

Every time I try to speak or apologize, she shuts me down.

For weeks.

"What have you done?" Edward finally asks as we stand by her door like forsaken statues.

"I was jealous of the boy." The words leave a sour taste in my mouth.

"You never learn, do you?"

"I have no idea how you stay this cold, Edward. Tell me it's not suspicious. Tell me you're not jealous, too."

"I know my place," he says under his breath. "She's the Queen. She can do as she wishes. Who am I to judge her?"

"So you don't mind if she's fucking him? And the other three who are about to join him in the *Art House*?" I whisper.

He closes his eyes, as if to process. Or is it

to push the image off his head? Or is it denial? "As long as I'm here, I'm thankful. Keep this attitude, and she'll replace us with her new secret army," he whispers back.

"What?"

"Why do you think she's told us to train them? Wake up, Sir Quinlan."

No.

She can't.

She won't.

The Art House is not solely about art anymore.

No!

"That's it. I'm going in."

He grabs my arm, his grip tight. "Do you have a death wish?"

"I can't stand another second of this shit. If she's going to replace me with some bastard, then I'm as good as dead."

I knock, take a deep breath and enter.

She's sitting by the window. "Did I tell you to come in?" She doesn't turn to face me.

I freeze for a second, my heart thrashing, but then I cross the room with fast strides until I kneel at her feet. "Forgive me."

She still doesn't glance at me.

"Majesty, it's been weeks. Please."

Silence lies between us like agony.

"I can't take another second of this treatment. Tell me what it's going to take to forgive me. I'm ready for anything."

Nothing. The room becomes so heavy with nothing I'm choking on it. "Majesty, I beg you."

"Please, get out, Sir Quinlan."

Pain slices through my heart. "I won't leave until you—"

"Until I what? Punish you?" She shifts her gaze toward me. "Fix you?"

"Yes," I whisper desperately.

"All those years, I've never taken you as a selfish man, Sir Quinlan. Now I see your true colors."

My eyes narrow in disbelief. "Selfish? I've denied myself everything to serve Your Majesty. To do what's best for *you*."

"Have you?"

I'm in awe she's even asking.

"The night you decided to be my escort and not my lover was a noble sacrifice on your side, completely selfless, wasn't it?

"Of course," I answer, perplexed. Why does she bring this up now?

She nods. "Let's prove it." She points at the curtains. "Close them and strip."

13.
HER MAJESTY

I prop my chin on my fingers as Quinn stands before me naked.

Perfect.

Defective.

The man who pretends to be my slave, when I am, in fact, his. Ten years of frustration and loneliness tear through me, rumbling like crushing waves.

Enough is enough.

I strip, too.

His mouth falls open. His look is dazed.

"I'm yours to take if you still want me," I say.

His lips and chin tremble. His gaze rakes me back and forth. "You know I do. More than anything. I just can't."

"Why not?"

"I'm your guard." He lifts a shoulder in resignation. "I took an oath to protect you at all cost. Even from myself."

"In this moment, you've never pledged yourself to the Royal Guards. There will be no legal consequences whatsoever. All your status privileges will remain the same. All you have to do is resign."

"What?"

"I'm making you the same offer I made you ten years ago. Resign now, and my body will be yours. Only yours."

His blinks, and his breathing accelerates. His lips are parting and closing as if he's about to say something but retracts at the last moment. Slowly, he moves closer until I feel the heat radiating from his body.

He places his hands on either side of my face and leans in for a kiss. I feel his chest, his heart banging violently against my palm.

All our suffering can end right this moment.

If he kisses me. If he finally takes me.

If he proves me wrong.

Do it, Quinn. Tell me I haven't been a fool all those years. Prove to me I am what you want. What you have always wanted.

His arm falls to his side, and he falls to his knees, tears spilling from his eyes. "I can't."

A heavy sigh seeps out of my mouth. "I didn't think otherwise." I put my clothes back on. "See, Sir Quinlan? You didn't do it for me; you didn't make that miserable choice because you were doing the right thing. You did it because you needed power more than love. Because you're a weak, hesitant man, who isn't willing to risk anything for the woman he says he loves."

"That's not true," he whimpers, grasping my feet. "I love you, I swear."

I kick him off me. The tip of my shoe pierces his abdomen. "Get the fuck out."

***

For the following month I find solace in Theodore's arms. The pain Quinn has left in my soul dulls when I'm with the boy, almost vanishes.

Almost.

But I look ahead to the future. To the prosperous, peaceful kingdom I've created and maintained. To the wedding of my son. To the happiness every other subject in the realm is willing to give me. To the three young men who have been more than enthusiastic to join the Art House. Drama free.

Having each one of the three for the first time has been a joyful experience. Having them together is even better.

For me. For the boys.

Definitely not for Theo.

He doesn't complain, but I can see it in his eyes.

When he's thrusting his cock between my

tits while one of the boys is taking me from behind. When I'm probing a boy's virgin rosebud with one gentle finger, and kissing the lips of another. When Theo doesn't know whether I'm moaning for him. Whether I'm coming for him.

I always reward him, though, with days of his own.

"When I have you all to myself I feel special," he says.

I smile. "You are special."

"Am I? The other three seem more *entertaining* to you."

"Only because they are controlled by their hormones." I chortle.

"You'd like me better if I didn't love you."

"Actually, Theo, I adore being loved by you." I press my naked body to his and feel his cock. "And being fucked by you. Your passion makes it so much better."

His mouth curves up. His shaft goes longer in my fist. His eyes linger on my lips.

"I know you still yearn for that kiss on the lips, but what if I give it to you somewhere else?"

His brows hook. His expression is a question. When I slide down and glance at his erection, he understands what I mean.

"Really? You'd do that?" He swallows.

"I've never done this before. Not even for the king. Perhaps it will show you how special you are to me."

He scratches the back of his head and grins. "Thank you."

I poise, stomach down, between his legs and start by licking him along the sides. Then I swallow his whole dick with my mouth. He bites his lips, his chest heaving, his whole body tense and burning. I suck him. Taste him. Move my lips up and down the length of his hard cock.

"Oh my God," he groans.

I release him for a second. "Tell me what you feel." Then I take him all in my mouth again.

"Fuck," he mumbles with his eyes closed. "I don't... It's fucking good. I feel... I feel your tongue deep inside, as if my dick didn't not stop at my pubis, but wound up inside me." He groans again. "I'm melting, yet I've never felt more hard."

I suck him deeper.

"Oh, Elysia. It's like my whole world reduced to Elysia's lips, Elysia's tongue." He squeezes his eyelids together, muscles clenching. He runs a hand through his hair, his head lolling back. "Oh God, I'm going to come."

I have his cock in my fist instead of my mouth, and he covers it with cum.

I gaze at his beautiful face, which is strained with the strength of his release, and smile. If I can do something like sucking his cock for his own gratification and take pleasure in the deed myself—something I've never done with another man, probably never will—means my feelings for Theo aren't sheer lust.

It means there's hope that one day I'll want to kiss his lips.

I'm looking forward to that day.

PART 3

HER MAJESTY & THE ESCORTS

1.
HER MAJESTY

I return from Timothy's wedding full of joy and pride. Our realm is bigger and stronger. My son has become a king.

My son is happy.

I'll be in an utter bliss, too, if I don't miss Theo's touch this much. If I don't have Quinn on my tail, breathing my air.

I've been deliberating with myself sending him to isolation for weeks. Sir Edward is more than capable of protecting me. Or I can assign any other guard. The Royal Guards are the best of the best.

But no matter how hard I try, I can't bring myself to do it.

My stupid heart still desires Quinn. I hate how much I still want to torture him, how much I still care.

I wish he'd injure himself so he's forced to retire—since he won't accept my offer and can't leave or quit without being sentenced to death. Perhaps when I stop seeing him day and night, I'll forget.

Heal.

I stroll down the garden for hours by myself to clear my head. When I'm tired, I rest in the solarium, gazing at the bright moon, making a wish.

Then I hear a crunch of leaves and a soft knock on the door. "Who dares interrupt me?"

"It's me, Your Majesty." Theo's voice streams softly through the glass door. Soothing. My beautiful slave. The virgin who has given up everything to please his Queen. The first member of my growing harem.

"Come in."

He enters, his smile bright under the moon.

"Why are you following me?" I ask.

"I saw Your Majesty walking alone without protection. I followed from a distance in case you needed me."

"In case I needed you to protect me?"

"Yes."

I smile and spread my hands. "Come here."

He takes my hands, kisses them and kneels in front of me. "I missed you."

"I missed you, too."

His arctic blue eyes sparkle. "How was the wedding?"

"Beautiful."

"Then why are you sad?"

"Because you weren't there with me. Next time I travel, I'm taking my *entertainers* along. You should start learning to perform, though. It'll be the perfect camouflage."

"That's very generous of you, Your Majesty, but seriously, what is troubling my Queen?"

"Have you grown this much to call me on my bluff, young man?"

"I wish you'd stop calling me that and see that I'm a man now. I also wish you'd trust me enough to confide in me."

My fingers stroke his raven black hair. "You know I trust you."

His arms stretch and fold around me. I rest my head on his, fighting the urge to cry.

"He's a great man, but he doesn't deserve you, Elysia."

I lean back and tilt his chin up with my finger. "Who?"

He half-smiles. "Sir Quinlan."

I purse my lips, not planning on convincing him he's wrong. There's no point denying it. "What gave me away?"

"It's not you. It's him." he says. "I had my doubts when you told me you saw and tortured the man you loved every day. It had to be one of your escorts. I didn't know whether it was Sir Edward or him. The way he

125

looks at you…and the awful way he looks at *me* confirmed my suspicions."

"He's threatened by you. He thinks you're going to take his place."

"Like I could."

"You don't want to be my escort. I have a strict no-fucking-my-guards rule."

A miserable shadow crosses his gaze. "You know what I mean."

I kiss him on the cheek, and then I look away. "I do."

"I don't want to make you sadder. I'm your entertainer, so let me entertain."

He makes me laugh. "I can't visit tonight."

"Then let's do it here." His eyes glint with mischief. "Now."

I grin. "What if someone sees us?"

"I doubt anyone will. But if it happens, you're the Queen. No one is going to harm you, and I'll take my chances."

"A risk taker you've grown to be?"

"I'll gladly risk my own life for just one smile from you."

"Oh, Theo." I sigh. "Keep that up and you might steal my heart after all."

His hands glide up my thighs, his teeth pearly against the moonlight. "I will."

A tingling spreads through me. "Is there something in particular you wish to do?"

"I felt your clitoris harden against my fingers before," he says. "Now I want to feel it harden against my tongue."

"That's a...very intriguing idea. But I have to warn you, I'm wearing undergarments."

"Then let's start by taking them off." His hands are faster than my permission.

I let him strip me off my bloomers. A light breeze tickles my uncovered skin. He stares at my bare sex, his tongue swiping along his bottom lip. "I'm going to eat your pussy, Your Majesty."

My stomach shakes with laughter. Then my eyes roll back as he unleashes a custom-made fire in my cunt with his tongue.

When his fingers come in play as well, I lose myself. He suckles me until he squeezes the last spasm of my pleasure, a wild flutter around his fingers, a release perfectly-timed.

"Happy?" He raises his head.

"Yes."

"Do you want more? Please say yes." His smile hangs midway. His face turns paler than the moon.

"What is it?"

"It's... Sir Quinlan." He gulps. "He's right outside, and he saw me."

Perfect.

"Don't be scared. You're under my

protection. He can't harm you," I assure Theo.

"That's not what I'm worried about." He shakes his head. "I was only trying to make you feel better. Now you're going to feel worse. That was never my intention, and I don't wish to cause any trouble between the two of you."

I smirk. "Is he still there?"

He nods.

My sadist demons kick in quickly as I remember a specific conversation I've had with Quinn.

About his wildest fantasies of me.

"Good," I say. "Now, I want you to tear my clothes apart, suck my tits till they hurt, lay me on my stomach and spank my ass as your cock fucks my pussy, long and hard."

Theodore stiffens.

"And I want you to look him in the eye the whole time."

2.

QUINN

I wish I were dead.

But I'm alive. Awake in my worst nightmare. Standing still. Even my heart seems to have ceased beating. Screaming on the inside, tears frozen in my eyes, I'm forced to watch my worst fear manifest.

Her eyes tear me to shreds.

Take her revenge.

You have broken me, Elysia.

For good.

Why am I still standing? Why haven't I collapsed yet?

Do I still relish her punishment? Is there any level of pain I can't take?

There is.

This.

Tim.

Tim.

Tim.

3.

QUINN

The trip back to her room is the longest I've walked.

There's no escape from the truth anymore.

Tonight, I do or die.

The second I'm alone with her, I summon all my courage and kiss her.

For ten years, I haven't touched those lips. That mouth that has kept me awake at night.

I taste it again. Devour it.

Melt in it.

Her palm rings against my temple.

I kiss her again.

She slaps me again.

I hug her.

She raps at me with her fists.

I capture both her arms and press her to me in a tight embrace. "I resign. Please take me."

"Get the fuck off of me."

I shake my head, holding her tighter. "Did you hear what I said? I'm done. I'll be yours,

Elysia. Just take me."

"My offer is no longer valid, Sir Quinlan. You're too late."

"More vengeance? What you've done tonight isn't enough?"

She knees me in the groin, forcing me to stumble back in pain. "Nothing will ever be enough."

"Why?! You know I love you!" I shout. "The only reason I haven't been with you is my fear that no one else will protect you like I would."

"Yes. Keep telling yourself that lie."

"It's the only truth there is! Haven't you asked yourself why the hell I never married? Had children of my own? Why I haven't even fucked any woman except the ones *you* told me to fuck for your own pleasure?"

"Perhaps you can't get it up unless I'm in the room. Who knows?" Her eyes pierce me. "Who cares?"

"You don't care about me anymore? You don't want me? You don't love me, Elysia?"

She folds her arms across her chest. "Good night, Sir Quinlan."

"Elysia—"

"Save your breath. Nothing you say or do will grant you your wish. What's done is done. You're old enough to deal with the consequences."

The words come crashing at me like a night ocean swell, coating everything in a bleak, drowning darkness.

Too loud, though. Deafening.

Maddening.

She's ripped my mind to shreds along with my heart. She's murdered the last flicker of hope I've had left.

You haven't only broken me. You have killed me, Elysia.

"You're too stubborn, too proud to listen." My chin lowers to my chest. My hands go limp. "As you please, Your Majesty." I gaze at her one last time. "Just know one thing, I've always loved you, and I shall love you till the day I die."

4.
HER MAJESTY

He hasn't slept a wink.

I can tell by the darkness of his expression. The grimness in his eyes.

The pain that has etched on his face overnight.

Good.

Let him suffer.

Burn.

For all the lonely nights.

The years.

The heartache.

Another Dispensation Day is here. I'm eager to see if there is going to be more potential apprentices for my Art House.

The next hour assures me there is.

The more the merrier.

And the best part is, the new boys who have joined already and this new one don't look like Quinn at all.

I will forget. I will heal.

After Dispensation is over, I go about with my day, make my decisions and send my messages. All today's realm affairs are attended to.

"If there's nothing else on the schedule, I shall take my afternoon stroll now," I tell my Chief of Ministers.

He kisses my hand. "Enjoy Your Majesty's afternoon."

"Actually, there is one matter left to handle," Quinn says, his voice thick.

Alarmed, I shift in my throne so I can see him.

He doesn't glance back.

"What is it, Sir Quinlan?" Chief asks.

Quinn leaves my side and steps down to the court.

My heart thuds with his every step until he stands before me, one thought in my head.

Theo.

Is he safe? Has Quinn harmed him?

This can't be. I've checked on him last night and this morning. I've even asked Edward to keep an eye on Quinn so he won't do anything stupid. I look at Edward for a hint, but he's as clueless as I am.

Quinn's gaze freezes on me for a few seconds that feel like an eternity. Then he unsheathes his sword, and goes down on one knee. "Forgive me, my Queen. Today is my last day in Your Majesty's service." He holds his sword on his palms and bends his head. "Today, I return my sword, and regretfully…quit."

My hand flies to my chest. My skin tingles, and a sudden coldness hits my core. This is worse than hurting an innocent man like Theo.

This is suicide.

"Are you…" My throat closes.

Are you out of your mind? This much of a selfish brat? A fucking coward?

You're leaving me? Are you this cruel, Sir?

This can't be happening.

"Look at me," I say under my breath. His bloodshot eyes hold me in place. The space between us fills up with empty static. My jaws tighten and flex as I summon the strength to speak again. "Are you aware of what you're saying, or have you been drinking too much, Sir?"

"I'm fully aware of what I said, Your Majesty."

If I were standing, I would collapse in my chair. If I were alone, I'd scream until I pass out.

"You will be charged with treason, Sir. You shall be stripped out of everything. You shall be tortured to death with no chance for mercy."

Please take back your words.

"I fully accept the *consequences* of my decision, Your Majesty."

Silence follows his words, and my throat closes even more. Quinn is clearly too hurt to think rationally. I need a loophole. An excuse. Anything.

Anything to spare his life.

I glance at Edward and the Chief of Ministers. Their eyes are sunken in their cavities. Helpless like I am.

I should just faint and put this madness on hold.

But what difference does it make?

God help me. What have I done?

Yes, I've hurt him, but that doesn't mean he kills himself. This merciless destiny has never been my intention for him.

I might be a sadist, but I'm not that ruthless.

Or am I?

A heartless monster that drives the ones who dare love her insane to the point of throwing themselves willingly in the cold abyss of death?

I breathe, but no air seems to come in. I close my eyes for a second, sifting through the rumbling chaos of emotions and thoughts inside me, and play my last card. "You shall be charged of negligence, Sir, for drinking on duty. You shall be—"

"I'm fully sober, and I willingly quit! The Laws of the Vow are clear, Your Majesty. Please. Just do what's right."

Lightheaded, I snap my eyes open. "Then you leave me no choice, Sir." I rise to my feet, my heart a million pieces scratching and tearing at my chest. "I regretfully declare Sir Quinlan…a traitor."

"Majesty," Edward gasps in shock.

I hold the arms of my throne to hide the shaking of my hands. "Chief of Ministers, do you witness?"

Speechless, his eyes wander between me and Quinn.

"Do you witness?!"

"Yes, Majesty."

I swallow my unshed tears. "Guards, please escort Sir Quinlan to the dungeon…where he awaits his execution day."

5.

QUINN

No regrets accompany me to the dungeon. Only the guards that were under my command a second ago.

One of them opens the iron gate of my new home for the few days I have left in my pathetic life. A dark cell that reeked of the smell of old blood and humidity.

A shiver runs through my body, but I don't *feel* cold or scared. I don't feel anything at all.

Numb from the inside out.

Perhaps I'm in too much pain to fathom that I've sentenced myself to death.

I bend and enter the foul cage. Nothing lights my way but the dim light of a fire torch one of the guards carries. I take one last glance at my jailers. My soldiers. My brothers. Their expressions are big question marks dark with blame and shock.

And sorrow.

The keys rattle in the fingers of the one who has opened the cell. He looks at me, shifting on his legs, his face tight. "I'm sorry,

Sir Quinlan."

"You're just doing your job, brother." I give a slight bow.

They all return the bow, and the iron gate screeches locked.

"For Her Majesty," they say in unison.

"For Her Majesty." Always and forever.

As their footsteps crunch the halls out of the dungeon, I inspect the four walls confining me. Dirty. Bare. Except for the shackles hanging from them. I wonder why I'm not in them already. Some sort of a special treatment?

My trained eyes wander around in the dark. There's nothing to sit on but the rough tiles of the floor.

I choose a corner and perch down. As I stretch my legs on the cold stone, my exhausted body awakens my numb soul, and a long, troubled, heated sigh breaks free from my chest.

I'm sorry my Queen. It's the only way.

To end my misery.

Yours, too.

I apologize for hurting you.

Today.

All those years when I thought I was doing the right thing.

Even though I still might be hurting you, it

will only be a moment, then it's gone for good. You have all these men to make you happy now. In a few days, I'll be just a memory. A bad one these men will help you forget.

I hope I've done the right thing this time.

6.
HER MAJESTY

"Find me a way out!" I barge into the consultation room, blood throbbing through my veins, Chief of Ministers behind me, Edward by my side.

The fire in my chest contrasts the stupid, soothing pastel colors dressing the room, and I want to set these velvet curtains and Persian rugs ablaze.

"Majesty, Laws of the Vow are Your Majesty's most solid and sacred laws. They are the base of the justice system in the kingdom. Your Majesty has never made an exemption, not even for yourself when you vowed never to marry again," Chief says the instance the doors are closed.

"I can't just let him die." My fist bangs the mahogany of my desk.

"Sir Quinlan is respected and loved by the entire realm, Your Majesty. No one wants him dead. However, breaking these particular laws now could cause confusion and feeling of injustice to the people. The kind of emotions that lead to disorder."

My teeth grind together as I sit behind the desk. Chief of Ministers is right. I don't need his reminder to know that. But I must save Quinn's life.

At any damn cost.

There has to be a way.

"Majesty, if I may ask, what drove Sir Quinlan to do such a terrible thing?"

I hear something in Chief's voice. Something I don't like and won't accept. Regardless of how correct it is.

Edward must hear the same thing as his hand has tightened around his sword. My eyes narrow with an unspoken warning at Chief. "I suggest you go ask him yourself and tell me the answer as I certainly do *not* have it, Sir."

Chief swallows and bows his head. "Of course, my Queen. I apologize. I was only asking in case Your Majesty might have noticed a change of behavior or deterioration in Sir Quinlan's state of mind recently."

Yes, I have, and it's all because of me.

I have driven him crazy.

I sigh and move around the desk, weighing the covert suggestion, my gaze stranded through the sparkling colored glass of the windows. "Do you think we should play that card?"

"I believe it's an option we should consider."

I amble to the windows, and he follows me. "If we get a physician to examine Sir Quinlan and determine he's not mentally fit to have made that fatal decision, Laws of the Vow won't apply to his situation, Majesty."

The option is worthy of consideration. If I declare Quinn a mad man, he will survive, which is the most important outcome for me at the moment.

An outcome I'm willing to sacrifice a lot to reach.

But what will the people say when they discover I've been protected by an incompetent escort?

Will they even believe it?

Can we make them believe?

Edward's footsteps march toward us. "With all due respect, Majesty and Chief, Sir Quinlan is not mad."

"I certainly hope so, Sir, because if he really is insane, and we free him, he might say things we shall all regret."

I spin around, arching a brow. It looks like I have so much more to be concerned about than convincing the people Quinn has lost his mind. "I don't like the implications hiding behind your words, Sir. If you know the reason behind Sir Quinlan's disgraceful behavior this afternoon, please, by all means, enlighten us."

He presses his lips for a moment before he dares speak. "I can assure you I don't know, my Queen. It's only a theory."

"What theory?"

"I don't think anything can make a wealthy, strong, levelheaded man such as Sir Quinlan commit such a desperate act…but a woman," he says. "A beautiful, powerful woman, my Queen."

Edward unsheathes his sword. "Choose your next words very carefully, Sir."

Chief takes a deep breath, his eyes wandering between Edward's menacing stare and the shining blade in his grip. Then he looks me in the eye. "Pardon me, Your Majesty, but it's my duty to alarm you of any threat or danger to the realm or you. Your Majesty knows that's all I care about." His gaze shifts toward Edward. "And I will gladly pay my life for it, if that's what it takes."

No doubt about it. This man has given his everything to the kingdom even before I was born. He's practically raised me to be the Queen I am today. If he thinks I should be alarmed, then I should be alarmed. "No one is questioning your loyalty, Chief." I give Edward a silent order to lower his sword. "But I believe it's you who's questioning my virtue."

"Your Majesty's virtue has never been questionable...yet." Chief steps forward. "But if Sir Quinlan speaks of this *woman*, Your Majesty's virtue will not be the only matter in question. It's your realm, my Queen, that will be in imminent danger."

7.
HER MAJESTY

My mind runs in circles, falling, rising, drowning, and spinning endlessly. Chief of Ministers is right about every word. If my people find out their Queen is a monster that plays with her men's hearts and bodies to satisfy her narcissistic, sadistic whims, they will no longer be my people.

I will lose everything.

It's either this or granting Quinn his wish. Become a murderer for the rest of my life.

NO.

My mind refuses to believe these are my only choices. Besides, Quinn will never hurt me. Not like this.

Yet the Quinn I know before last night isn't the desperate Quinn who has condemned himself to a torturous death…

I don't recall how I've reached my chamber. All I know is that the second I'm alone inside, I will collapse. "Edward, stay with me. I don't wish to be left alone."

He bows in obedience.

"Tell the guards not to disturb me for any reason and lock the doors," I add.

"As you wish, Majesty." He bows again and executes my commands.

I take a seat by the window bay. He stands next to me. Silence accompanies us for a while, each of us tumbling in bleak thoughts, dreary as the gray winter sky outside. "Do you hate me now?" I murmur.

More silence.

My heart squeezes. "Of course. You have every right."

"No, Majesty. I apologize for not answering right away. I was...taken aback. I mean..." He squats next to my chair, and I glance at him. His bright silver eyes penetrate me. "Your Majesty knows exactly how I feel, and that will never change. Can never change, even if I want to."

Studying his beautiful face, I hope for a different answer even if I don't deserve it.

I don't hate you. I love you. All of you. Demons and flaws and all.

But who would love a monster for being a monster?

Edward doesn't hate me because, like all my men, he's under my spell. The spell of beauty and power.

The royal supremacy spell.

147

Queen Elysia's spell.

He loves me against his will.

He can't help it. He's a man after all.

My palm joins his cheek in a caress. "Are you going to leave me, too, Ed?"

A painful grimace contorts his face. "Never, my Queen." His lips print a soft kiss inside my hand as his eyes close. "Never."

"You should." I retract my hand. "I don't wish for you to meet the same destiny as his."

His eyes snap open, a flicker of panic across them. Then he kneels. "This is my destiny, Majesty. My vow."

"He's taken the same vow before you."

"Perhaps. But in my heart, I've vowed to serve Your Majesty without limits or expectations. To be anything you want me to be." He crawls to my feet, lifts them and put them on his back. "This, here, is where I belong."

Having Sir Edward on all fours as a footstool, surprisingly, doesn't make me feel any better. However, a flood of emotions invades me. I can no longer resist my tears.

"Oh, Majesty." He rests my feet on the carpet and sits up. "Please, don't."

I look away. "I'm in so much pain, Ed. More than I can bear at the moment."

"I know I can't take the pain away, but I'll

do anything to lessen it." He moves on his knees to meet my gaze. The back of his fingers brushes off my tears. "Command me, please. Tell me what to do. I'm at your disposal, my Queen."

His hot breath rolls across my skin, and, in this instance, I don't have the internal strength or the necessary sanity to fight the desire to lean into him and press my lips to his.

When my eyes fasten to his mouth, he gulps. He appears to be fighting the same urges, but this is a threshold of intimacy that we should never cross.

Especially not at the current circumstances, when a man very dear to our hearts is about to lose his precious life without a way of saving it, and I might be labeled a whore Queen not only till the day I die but in history as well for indulging in affairs such as the ones I'm about to pursue.

Yet pain is a vicious master. The most dominant. Once it's here, one must serve until it leaves. Whatever it takes. With no regard to anything whether it matters or not.

"Help me feel something else." My hand moves at its own will, settles on his nape and pulls him into a kiss.

He shivers, searing heat spreading through

his body and through my fingers. His mouth doesn't respond at first, but then it closes over mine, and I moan, sinking back into my chair.

Who the hell kisses like this?

I don't know if it's the nature of the situation or the depth of our ache that intensifies this moment, but these lips, sharp and cleanly defined, yet fuller than I expect, kiss in a way that scorches any and all of my nerve endings.

Moaning again, my fingers plunge into his blond hair. God, it's so soft I fear yank at it in case it comes off in my fist. His hands find my arms and stay, their warmth seeping through the fabric of my sleeves. I pull away to reclaim the breath he's taken away and gauge his reaction.

His eyes, dark clouds now, heavy-lidded, gaze upon me with familiar hunger. A blush suffuses the poor man's skin.

A sigh quivers inside my chest and out of me. "You possess a sort of passion that beats my expectations, Sir."

"A sort I only have for you, my Queen, but I must know how to hide my emotions well and show them only when Your Majesty bids them free," he whispers.

"Have you learned nothing from your friend?"

"I fear so, Majesty."

I press my lips in sorrow. "Are you aware that the only thing I wish to do with that kind of passion is abuse it to the point of destruction?"

"Well aware." His thick lashes cast a shadow over his cheeks as his gaze meets my feet and the floral pattern of the carpet. "Yet I welcome it to the point of begging for it."

"You're a fool, Sir."

"Your Majesty is absolutely right. In your presence, we *all* are nothing except foolish slaves." He looks at me again. "Accordingly…may I suggest Your Majesty take your humble slave to the playroom to hurt and abuse as much as it takes to ease the pain?"

8.
EDWARD

I'm not only a fool.

I'm a traitor.

A man, a brother, with whom I've shared everything for a decade is going to be tortured to death—because of her—and all I'm thinking about is that kiss and what awaits in the clandestine room.

The pain squeezing my heart, almost splitting it in half, evaporates the second our lips connect. The years of brotherhood and honor eradicated for an hour in her arms.

That's what she does to a man. Carve him hollow until there's nothing left but her to fill that void she's created. Until he believes beyond doubt he can't live without her even if he tries.

Until she owns him.

Body. Heart. Mind. Soul. Everything.

A fool indeed.

A lowlife that deserves the excruciating pains she will inflict without mercy.

She delights in wielding power over men in

domination, where pleasure, pain and humiliation may be enjoyed combined, and I delight in the sweet surrender to her.

My Queen. My owner.

In the playroom, she strips me of my clothes and humanity. A collar with a metal leash circles my neck, and then *she* circles my naked body, assessing it as a lioness might survey its prey.

She twirls the chain around her fingers and pulls me to her face. "Kiss me again."

Once more I touch the royal lips, languorously, savoring every moment as if it's the last, dazed that I'm alone with Her Majesty after all those years. My forbidden fantasies are alive in this secret chamber, where others have pleased her before while I've watched and guarded.

I shall please her now. All by myself.

Suddenly, her sharp teeth hold my lower lips between them and spear it bloody.

My eyes widen. "Ahh…Ah…Aw…"

When she draws back, she licks her lips, tasting my blood. The glint of satisfaction in her eyes cloaks the pain in my mouth and sets a smile there.

"Now undress me," she orders as she loosens her grip.

"Yes, Majesty." I obey, a slight shake in my

hands when I unbutton her bodice. I help her out of her skirt and petticoat. Fumbling, I untie the ribbon at the top of her undergarment, and it drops.

So many times I have seen her naked. But now her perfect body that I'm allowed to watch but never touch is now exposed before me.

Only me.

She removes the pins in her head and let her hair, a waterfall of fire, cascade over her porcelain landscape: across her abundant hills and downwards, to the mysterious valley between her legs.

The thrill of anticipation causes my penis to leap. At the same time, a sick part of me hopes that the other gentlemen who have had the honor of serving her are here to feel some of the envy I've long had for them.

Her strong tug at my leash brings me to my knees. "Lick me from the foot upward."

"With pleasure." I start with the toes and suck between them. The soles. The heels. Then my tongue glides up her ankles. Her calves. The area behind her knees. Her thighs. She's so incredibly soft I want to devour her.

Not without permission, of course.

I glance up at her as I pause under the pink of her sex.

She parts her legs and inclines her head with unspoken approval.

I lick my lips at this stirring sight before I enter her with the tip of my tongue. My eyes roll back with pleasure as I locate the waiting nub and taste her for the first time. With a sharp intake of breath, I sip Her Majesty's wet cunt.

My stare lifts to her to see if she's enjoying herself. She meets me with a look I've seen before. Many times. A look I've long yearned to see in her eyes for me. The one she gives her prey before she's about to pounce.

Her toes kick my testicles, and I moan inside her. Then she grabs the chain so tightly, strangling me. Pressure presses my skull. Heat floods my face as I gasp for air.

"I didn't say you may stop." She kicks me again.

I groan loudly and push my mouth into her. My eyes roll back again, this time, while I suffocate. I know she won't kill me, still it feels like I'm going to die. There's an inexplicable kind of thrill in approaching death. Terrifying yet arousing. My veins and my phallus will explode.

She steps backwards, bidding me some air, but she doesn't loosen the collar. A wild cough takes over me. Involuntary tears spill from the corners of my eyes. Dragging me, she orders me on my back.

I lie on the cold marble, and she drops the leash. With one swift move, she twirls and sits on my face. "Eat my ass."

My nose and my mouth dive in her asshole. How strange and wicked it is that I can barely breathe, yet my erection is getting longer by the second? Does she like the sight of it while she's smothering me with her sweet buttocks? God I want to be buried between them forever.

"You have a big cock, Ed," she says, and I feel her fingers wrapping around the shaft. My pelvis grinds up reflexively. "Do you think it will please me better than your tongue?"

Oh dear God.

I wish I could speak. I wish I could do many things. But all I can do is *eat her ass.* Until she commands me differently.

She spins on her heels, my penis still in her fist, and pulls my head into her other opening. "Lick me hard."

"Yes, Majesty." I do as she says, her hard nipples in my face, her wicked nectar flowing in abundance.

She holds my gaze as I drown between her nether lips, her fist rubbing my erection. "You can't come."

I blink. Repeatedly. How can I not come? She's naked on top of me, stroking my already-engorged erection, and my mouth is devouring her sex. How can I not come?

"Please, Majesty, have mercy on me," I say between licks. "It's my first time serving Your Majesty this intensely."

She smiles, moaning. "If you spill your disgusting seed in my hand, you'll be severely punished."

I grimace. "Yes, Majesty."

Struggling so hard not to enjoy myself, I close my eyes. Perhaps if I think about how I'm nothing but a toy for her, another bitch in her harem, I won't find this as pleasurable as it is.

No.

In fact, unlike Quinn, seeing her with other men doesn't bother me. It's that *I* can't be with her that does. I don't mind being another bitch in her harem at all. I might even enjoy the ménage if I'm a participant.

I must think about something else because pre-cum is leaking out of me already.

My eyes squeeze shut, but I can't block the sounds of her moaning from my ears. I moan, too, suckling her tormenting wetness. "I beg you, Majesty. Let me come, please."

She giggles. "No."

Her laughter, humiliating, yet heart-fluttering, along with her strokes drive me to the edge. "I'm very sorry, my…Queen." My cum raptures in her fist.

Her Majesty tsks. "I warned you if you came, I'd punish you severely."

"I'm aware, Majesty," I say, still recovering from the forte of my release. "I'm so deeply sorry to have disappointed you."

She brings her stained hand to my mouth. "Lick it clean."

My body stiffens, nauseated. Nevertheless, disobeying her twice in a row will upset me more than any of the discomfort and disgust I will feel as I lick my own cum.

Slowly, the lips that have just tasted her wonderful secretions suck this disgusting, creamy white liquid off her fingers. The act is so humiliating and sickening that I feel like an animal, yet I feel a surge of arousal at the control she exerts over me; Her Majesty is a woman to be feared and admired simultaneously.

I almost gag, but I don't quit until I finish the task. The look on her face and the juices that still spill on my chest assure me of her content.

"Good boy." She rises to her feet. "Go clean yourself and return to receive the rest of your punishment."

9.
HER MAJESTY

From a trunk placed to one side, I fetch a leg spreader. This I place between his ankles when he returns, fixing them apart, so that he stands not uncomfortably, but rather self-consciously, his genitalia swinging free. I bind his wrists in front of his body with a sash of velvet.

"You have me tied in all sorts of knots, my Queen," he says.

I give him one of my charming smiles and fetch a pair of silk gloves and another toy. The cat. Edward stiffens in alarm when he sees the multi-tailed leather whip.

"You disobeyed me." I flick my weapon lightly at his generous cock. The fringed tail end makes contact with the tender skin, but his face remains immobile. I wield the whip a little harder, catching him full along the length of the shaft. He stands firm, unmoving, except for his cock. The whip lashes twice more, each time raising the beast between his legs. The spasms in my pussy twitch hard.

"Are you hurting?" I ask, the sound of my lashes high.

"Yes, Majesty," he answers, his bound hands balling into fists. "So much."

"You deserve to be punished."

"Yes, Majesty, please. Thank you."

"Would you like me to hurt you some more?"

"Yes! Hurt me." He gazes at me with urgency in his expression and voice. "Hurt me until I can't stand it anymore. I deserve nothing but to be punished by you, my Queen."

His words set my inner demons loose. I bid him turn. His blond ass begs for a different color. Shades and shades darker.

I command him to bend and part his legs, so that his testicles hang, huge and low. The whip lashes land on them now, and he can't hold his groans any longer. When his knees hit the floor, I use my toy on his strong ass. The muscles ripple and contract with every lash. The stoic soldier falls to pieces. His squirms, screams and the heavy marks on his buttocks beg me to stop, but he hasn't uttered a word.

"If you wish me to stop, you know what to do," I prompt.

"I do." He moans, sweat covering his

statuesque body. "But I don't wish Your Majesty to stop."

I don't wish to stop either. Even though my sex is dying for release, the pain I'm dying to obscure isn't fading.

At all.

The cat drops on the floor. The gloves cover my hands. I reach down and grasp his balls, kneading them gently. His bound fists bang the marble as his groans echo in the sacred chamber.

I press them harder, gushes of desire streaming between my thighs. His pain is evident, but so is mine.

My hand clenches for what seems an eternity, Edward begs for mercy. I finally let go, yet the heavy rock pressed on my chest won't.

"Are you all right?" I ask, moving to his front to see his face.

He bites his teeth into his upper lip, trying to hold back a sob, nodding slowly.

"I already know how much you want to please me. How far you're willing to go to show me you're mine. You have nothing to prove, Ed."

He nods again. "Thank you, but I need this…as much as you do, Majesty."

The back of my silk-gloved hand brushes

his cheek. A small, aching smile touches his lips.

"At least, tell me it's fulfilling for you. Is it out of you yet? Has the physical pain masked the one inside?"

"Part of it, yes. Hasn't it for Your Majesty?"

"I fear not."

"Then I beg you to do whatever it takes, Majesty. I'm all yours."

I tap him on the shoulder and return to do what I've intended to do with the gloves. If this doesn't satisfy me…

I grasp the firm ass cheeks, allowing a draught of cool air to move between them. As his anus is exposed, he clenches his buttocks, inspiring a firmer grip from me.

"Plugs, Majesty?" he inquires, panicking.

"No." My smallest digit slithers inside his ass. "Fingers."

His groans are different now.

Sounds of undoubtable pleasure.

"You're tight," I say.

"Nothing has ever…been there before, Majesty."

An ass virgin.

Interesting.

After having Theo, I've developed a special affinity for anything virgin. Let's see if Sir

Edward will moan with pleasure still with two fingers inside.

"Ah… Oh…God," he murmurs.

"Do you like it, Ed?"

He pauses. "I think I do, Majesty."

Both my fingers slide in and out his anus with a fast rhythm, his sharp groans a delightful chorus.

My third finger finds its way in but not without a struggle on his side and force on mine.

"I don't think I can take any more, Majesty."

"I thought you liked it."

"I do…but it's burning like hell now."

"Do you wish me to stop?"

He looks at me over his shoulder for a moment, then he shakes his head.

My fingers enter and exit him a few more times, stretching his hole, before my index finger joins the fun.

The loyal protector screams like a bitch in heat, quivering, as I fingerfuck his virgin ass. I wish to fist him, but I'm certain I'll injure him. No one takes a fist on their first time.

I laugh a little, enjoying the sight of this mighty man, bent on the floor, legs spread, ass dark red with my marks, four fingers up his guts.

Yet what's eating my soul hasn't had enough. It won't sleep.

Why is it failing? The pain inside me is more powerful than my power. Causing more pain shall not conquer it. I need something else. Something stronger.

10.
HER MAJESTY

I remove my gloves and the leg spreader, bring some water and walk toward him. He empties the glass in one gulp and sighs in relief, resting his abdomen on the floor.

"You may use the bed in this room. Do you need help getting up?" I offer my hand.

He takes it and lifts himself upright as best as he is able. "Thank you, Majesty."

I escort him to the king-sized bed on the other end of the room. When he sits, he hisses, aching, and immediately jumps to his feet.

"Lie on your front." I help him on the crimson bedspread, the marks on his ass darker.

He settles on his stomach and spreads his arms before him, his eyes closed in pain. "Have I failed you, Majesty?"

Resting next to him, I gaze at him even if he can't see me admiring the gold of his hair, the plane of his jaw, and the breadth of his shoulders. "It's not you who have failed me."

The silver in his eyes shines at me. "Your Majesty loves him too much?"

I pick the bitterness in his tone easily. "I've never thought you're a jealous man. Certainly not at such harsh times."

"I shock myself as well, Your Majesty. My feelings today are beyond my comprehension. It all happened too fast this afternoon. I felt as though I was in a bad dream, waiting impatiently to wake up. Then…" he says, too ashamed to fully meet my eyes now.

I scowl. "Then I kissed you, and the bad dream switched into a more delightful one."

"The most delightful of them all. It is *the* dream. The one I live my entire life for, even if I know it will never come true. Not with the Art House, and certainly not with Sir Quinlan around." His brows hook. "I'm not a jealous man, Majesty, but I'm certain I wouldn't be here, *the dream* wouldn't have come true unless…"

A lump rises to my throat. This is a new level of evil that even I can't endure. I've turned men, brothers, against each other, wishing each other dead.

My lips part with a silent moan. "I'm sorry I didn't express how special you are to me that you'd feel that terrible way toward your friend's calamity. Perhaps what you assumed is true. I might have loved him more than I should have, but I've set my mind to forget him. Then he does this…dishonorable act, and all I can think about is him. I can't even relish the beauty of what you've given me today."

"You should never apologize, Majesty. I'm the only one to blame here, and I despise myself for how I felt and behaved. I'm fully aware that Your Majesty will never see me as I wish to be seen. I'm nothing to you." His shoulders lift in resignation. "But I can't help myself. I'm a pathetic disgusting animal."

"That's not true, Ed."

"Yes, it is, but it doesn't matter. What matters is that I'm unsucceeded in giving Your Majesty a shred of relief after all. I truly wish there was something I could do to make Your Majesty feel better. At least, my betrayal wouldn't be for nothing."

My fingers thread the soft locks of his hair. "There's something I'd like to try if you have any strength left."

He rises on his elbows, vigorous as if I haven't laid a hand on him. "Anything for my Queen."

I cup his face with my hands. "Inflicting pain has never failed me until today. If it can't fight these gut-slicing aches inside me, then nothing will ever do."

"I don't understand, Majesty."

"I've been fighting the wrong feeling. It's not pain that I must defeat. It's the love that caused it all. And I'll fight it with more love." I lean closer. "Kiss me, Ed. Make love to me like a man does a woman. Like you've always dreamed."

He gapes at me. "What about Your Majesty's rules? It's one thing Your Majesty plays with me, but…" His gape changes into a long, lustful stare at my naked body. He must be picturing what I've just offered him to do with it. Then his eyes squeeze shut. "And Chief's concerns?"

"If I'm going down anyway, then fuck the rules."

"You're not going down, my Queen."

"Maybe, but if you obey me now, if you *fuck* your Queen, you will be going down with me, too. Does it scare you? Because if it does, you're free to walk away."

"No!" He shakes his head quickly. "No." A grin stretches his lips, already approaching.

"Then show me those beautiful fantasies. Make me feel something else, Ed."

"Oh, Majesty." His lips connect with mine with the same passion that has taken my

169

breath away earlier. And more.

He smells of desire and sweat and masculinity. Amazing. When he lies on top of me, a chill runs through my spine despite the heat of his body. I welcome his weight upon me, the feel of it solid and sinewy.

He suckles me, his lips and mouth pulling on my skin. I close my eyes and ease in his arms. His fingers rove up and down my body, feeling my breasts, my waist, my belly, my hips, my thighs, everything.

I open my eyes and glance down, tracing the thin line of hair beneath his navel that pointed toward his cock, and I see it glistens with excitement, ready.

I, too, am more than ready.

But he doesn't penetrate me yet. Gently, he spreads my thighs and buries his nose inside me. "Your Majesty's smell is divine." Then he cups my pussy and uses his whole tongue. "And Your Majesty's taste…" A warm sigh blows on my vulva causing me to wriggle.

I lift my legs so that it's better placed to accept the ministrations of that kindly mouth, which sips so attentively at my damp cunt. It's not long before my slick clitoris reveals I don't wish to wait any longer. "Now, Ed."

His silver eyes blaze at my command. He adjusts himself over me, resting his elbows on either side of me. I hold his face between my hands. At a final nod from me, he inches within. I stifle a scream of arousal.

His chest heaves, and his eyes roll back. When he looks at me again and commences his pumping in worthy fashion, I watch him. In his face, I see tenderness as well as lust. I see care.

Unmistakable love.

A different kind than the helpless one I watch in Theo's young eyes. Or the angry, tormented kind Quinn gives me.

In Ed's expression, I see unhesitant, mature amour that is willing to give and not take.

Sacrifice that is offered with content.

I gasp audibly and throw back my head as his prowess meets with my approval. My breasts jump and fall with each thrust. My body unfurls, resonating with new vibrancy.

He lashes harder, lifting my rump to allow the deepest angle of entry. His hands imprison my hips as he fucks with energy indefatigable. His eyes turn darker than ever, glittering in an otherworldly manner. His mouth is open, forming words he can't utter. He's about to lose all control, I feel it.

"Make me come, Ed. Then come inside me." I swallow, transfixed by each measured penetration and withdrawal, lost in my own desire.

He speeds up, the exertion in his voice and the sweat coating his incredible body drive me insane. My walls clench and releases around him. I give full voice to my fulfillment, a melody echoed by his roar of release.

Breathless, he slumps over me and finishes this beautiful intercourse as he's started it. With a passionate kiss.

"I feel so much more for you now, Ed," I say. "More than I've thought I would...or could."

His gaze locks with mine as he brushes the moist locks of my hair off my forehead. "I love you, my Queen."

His words sound more of a confession than a statement. As if it's the first time he's ever said it, even to himself.

I smile.

"Does this gorgeous smile mean I've succeeded this time?"

11.
EDWARD

"Do you think Quinn would do what Chief worries he would? Do you think he would hurt me like this, as another kind of punishment, if I don't allow his stupid charade and save him?" Her Majesty asks.

I chuckle. This is not what I've been waiting to hear. Not at this moment.

"Why are you laughing? There's nothing humorous about what I said, Sir," she says as I roll off of her.

"Of course, not, Majesty. I do apologize. I was rather…surprised." I get out of the bed, a surge of anger burning me. "May I get dressed, please?"

"Ed," she holds my hand, "speak to me. What's on your mind?"

"It's not my place, Majesty, but it hurt me, mentioning him now when I've been trying so hard to make you forget about him even for a few hours. Especially when we all know he's neither insane nor capable of hurting Your

Majesty."

"So what he did today is an act of sanity and not hurtful to me at all?" she exclaims.

"It's an act of desperation and hurting oneself. Your Majesty can't possibly believe that he's punishing you."

"What are you saying?"

I throw my hands in the air with exasperation. "Sir Quinlan is only punishing himself for losing you to the bastard, Majesty."

Sitting up, she stares at me with fury blazing in her eyes.

"I'm sorry for raising my voice, Majesty, but this is the truth. He curses himself for hesitating when Your Majesty gave him the chance to be with you. And when he heard Your majesty wasn't in love with him anymore…"

"Did you know anything about his obscene plan?"

"I swear I did not," I answer, regret tearing through me. "But I should have noticed, and I should have stopped him."

Her gaze tears away from me. Her legs swing free off of the bed. "I should have, too. His last words to me last night were loud and clear, but he was right. I am too stubborn and too proud to listen." Her fists press the silk sheets as she looks at me over her shoulder. "We have to save him, Ed."

"We shall, Majesty. May I suggest something, though?"

She nods.

"Sir Quinlan is very stubborn, too, blinded with rage…and love. If we intervene, he might do something even extremer."

"Like what? Tell the world about my sexual deviance? I'd rather take my chances."

I shake my head. "I fear if we force him out, he might…"

"Might what, Edward? Speak!"

The muscles around my heart squeeze sharply. "Take matters into his own hands, Majesty."

12.
HER MAJESTY

I call Chief of Ministers to an urgent meeting this evening. Quinn's matter must be resolved.

Today.

After Edward shares his concerns in the consultation room, Chief's expression assures me he understands the gravity of the situation.

Chief takes a few moments to think. "How about, in the spirit of the upcoming Holiday season, Your Majesty applies the act of mercy on Sir Quinlan's execution day?"

"Traitors are tortured to death then executed without a chance for mercy. My Laws of the Vow are clear. I've never made an exception." I pace the room like a caged lioness.

"Under the circumstances and the sentiments of the holidays, I'm certain the people will understand and encourage it."

"That's a fine idea only if Sir Quinlan *asks* for mercy," Edward taunts.

"What are you suggesting, Sir?" Chief

crosses his arms over his chest as my heart thrashes and a heavy pulse throbs in my skull.

"The decision to be saved needs to come from Sir Quinlan himself." Edward looks at me. "Let me speak to him, Majesty. I think I know how to convince him."

"And if you fail?" The pitch of my voice is higher than I intend.

"Majesty, please, calm down," Chief says.

"Don't tell me to calm down, Sir! If Sir Edward fails and Sir Quinlan is triggered or alarmed, he might kill himself in his cell before we have a chance to rectify the situation. No physician or mercy would pardon him then."

The men's eyes follow me as the place shrinks in silence.

Neither of them can understand how I feel. Neither of them is the woman because of whom an innocent man is going to lose his life. Chief and Edward are not the murderers here.

I am.

I'm the one who started it, and I'm the one who's going to finish it.

No one can save Quinn but me.

13.
QUINN

Two days have passed with nothing for company but the occasional guard who brings in the meals and the excruciating memory of her and the bastard.

I should have been processed by now with an execution date set, but nothing happened.

Why?

She's never patient with traitors. Breaking the Vow is an act of defiance, to her before it is for the law. She doesn't tolerate it.

That's why I did it. To end my suffering quickly. So why, Elysia? What am I still doing here?

"More vengeance? What you've done tonight isn't enough?"

"Nothing will ever be enough."

Our conversation that night plays in my head over and over. She's tortured my heart. My body will be tortured on execution day. Now, she's leaving me to rot to torture my mind.

You're so cruel, my Queen.

And so beautiful.

I sigh, resting the back of my head against the rough wall, my knees bent to my abdomen. God I miss her. For ten years I've seen her, talked to her, walked with her every day and night. I wish I could see her one more time before the execution day. To tell her how much I love her one last time. How much I yearned to make her happy.

How sorry I am that I didn't.

Steady footsteps ring in the halls, stalking to my cell. Is it time? She's finally letting me rest?

I look up through the iron bars, guards' faces forthcoming. One of the soldiers is holding a chair. When they reach the cell, they soldiers step aside, and I scamper to my feet.

"Majesty," I gasp.

Her eyes fix me in place as her red cloak sweeps the floor toward the iron gate. "Open the cell and leave us."

One guard uses his key. Another places the chair inside. She enters, and he shuts the gate behind her, hand her the keys and leaves with the rest.

She stands still, her gaze arresting, while my heart pounds violently against my ribs. I wish I could throw myself into her arms and ask her to let me cry on her bosoms. Perhaps she can read it in my eyes. How sorry I am to have defied her—betrayed her as she would call it. Perhaps she'll understand how hopeless I am that I had no choice but to do what I did.

Her gaze doesn't soften, though. The longer I stare into her eyes, the weaker my knees go. Until they hit the rough floor.

With my head bent, I hear her sigh as her cloak brushes my knees. Towering over me like this, I feel so small in her presence, my breathing loud, shivering. "Please, say something, Majesty."

She spins, slipping the keys into her pocket, and sits on the chair. "Your execution day has been pushed to the Holiday season."

My head jerks up. "What? No, Majesty, please. That's a week from now."

"So?"

My eyes widen. "So please stop punishing me, I beg you. Waiting to die is worse than death itself. Extending my stay in solitude like this would madden me."

"Madder than you already are?"

I bite my lips, waves of rage and despair roiling inside me.

"It's one way to save your sorry ass. I can't execute a mad man," she says.

"Majesty knows I'm not insane, and I know

Majesty doesn't wish to save me, only punish me."

"You're a foolish prick," she says under her breath and leaves her chair. "Sir Edward tells me you did what you did to punish yourself. Is that true?" She sweeps the cell with her eyes, ambling around.

I purse my lips, head bowed. "Yes, Majesty."

"Are you not aware that there are other punishments more enjoyable than breaking your vow?" She stops, and I can feel her eyes on me. "Than leaving me?"

The blame and pain dripping from her voice tear at my heart. *But you hurt me, too, my Queen.* "I am aware, but I don't deserve the joy, Majesty…or the honor of serving you and staying by your side."

"That was for me to decide."

I lift my head to see the gorgeous face I've missed terribly. The face that hurts and haunts me till the day of my demise. Perhaps after that, too. "Then I apologize for yet another mistake, Majesty. I am a foolish prick after all. I surely hope the joy Your Majesty receives watching the executioner slice me open and cut me to pieces, is enough price to pay for all of my mistakes and the nuisance I've caused you through the years."

She roars in anger and swoops down on me. Her hands wrap around my neck. "I should kill you now and get it all over with."

My stare doesn't leave hers as she clogs my wind pipes. Struggling to breathe, I tense, all my blood rushing to my groin.

For heaven's sake, how sick am I?

The cell spins around me, and I feel as if I'm about to lose all consciousness. "Majesty," I rasp.

"Aren't you so eager to die?" She presses my throat harder. "Fucking die, you son of a bitch."

Reflexively, my hands fist around hers, pulling them off of me. "Majesty, please."

"Fuck!" She releases me at last.

I fall on my side, hand on my chest, gasping for breath, coughing madly. She towers over me again until I recover. Her index finger touches my chin, lifting my face to her. The way she looks at me makes me tremble.

"You're a coward. Always have been." She spits on my face.

I flinch but don't look away. She slaps me. I don't dare move. She does it again and again. I wait it out, welcoming it.

Yes, the bravest man in the kingdom is a coward when it comes to love, my Queen.

Your love.
And we both know why.
One man can never fill your heart.
I shall never be enough.

She grabs me by the collar of my shirt and presses me to the wall. I'm out of breath again, this time because I can feel the warmth of her body on mine. Our chests heave together. Our lips inch dangerously close.

"God damn you." She closes the distance between our mouths and seals it with a kiss.

I kiss her back, grinding against her so she knows how hard my desire is for her. Suddenly, hesitation flees me. No more fear or obligation. No more thinking. Nothing more to lose.

Our bodies move, fueled by rage, lust and…love.

I push the cloak off her shoulders and spread it on the floor. She smirks in ridicule.

Her palms push my chest to the wall. Shackles rattle from the impact. "Strip," she orders.

I've given up hope that I could ever feel this way again. Excited. Terrified. Aroused.

By her.

I remove my clothing without embarrassment or concern. Once naked, I stand expectantly. "My body is at your disposal, my Queen."

She inspects me from head to toe, her eyes lingering on my erection. Her fingers untie the top of her dress and work the buttons of her bodice. Anticipation builds on my desire as I yearn to see her naked perfection once again. The dress pools around her ankles, and she steps out of it.

As her plump flesh touches me, a long, heated sigh breaks free from my chest and onto the fiery curls, ruffling the careful arrangement off her forehead. "May I please touch you?"

She smiles and holds my wrists, leading them somewhere. Hopefully, her breasts that are teasing my ribs with their erect nipples.

Her wet tongue swipes across my lower lip then the upper one, my mind numb, my will abducted. Then I feel them.

Cold, rusty metal surrounds my wrists.

Her smile turns into a grin as she steps back. My heart speeds up. Sweat breaks out along my forehead and for a minute the world seems like it's spinning and yet I am still. I'm standing in the middle of crazy, without a clue what this gorgeous devil has in mind.

"What are you doing, Majesty?"

"What does it look like I'm doing?" She bends down and chains my ankles, too.

When she straightens up, she moves backwards, her eyes glistening with mischief. "Now you may touch me."

I move as fast as I can, but my chains allow me this much distance. My hands stretch as far as they can, spreading my fingers in vain. I tug at the shackles, but my attempts are only disappointments.

Her amusement isn't hidden. She enjoys having me robbed off my dignity, caged like a wounded animal, shackled and desperate for her touch like this.

To think that I finally have broken free from her enslavement when *I* set a termination date on the servitude called life…

Whom am I fooling? Here I am, at her mercy once again.

When will I ever learn?

Apparently never.

Queen Elysia's slave till the day I die.

14.
HER MAJESTY

I take my time, watching as his lips and balls turn blue. The cell is cold, but I'm burning, a sweet pressure aching between my legs.

Humiliation. Obsequiousness.

Love and hate combined.

All in the expression of one man.

My man.

Whether he likes it or not.

I moan internally.

When he is convinced the shackles are stronger than himself, his gaze falls to the floor, broken. "Please tell me you're not going to leave me like this till my execution day."

"Don't put tempting ideas in my head." I rest on the chair.

His eyes, dark with humiliation and need, rise to meet me. "Would you please tell me what your real intentions with me are?"

"Scared?"

He lets out a long breath, the struggle with his pride clear and priceless. "I must say yes,

Majesty."

I stand and saunter toward him. "My intentions are completely dishonorable, Sir."

"My God," he murmurs, biting his lips.

With precise calculations, I bring myself within his reach. The shackles jingle all at once, and his hands are around my waist in a tight embrace, his lips on my mouth, the kiss slow and lingering, his tongue lazy, meticulous. "I'm not going to wait for permission any longer," he breathes in me, his smell terrible, yet somehow arousing, his palms sliding up to my breasts.

"Good boy. Rebellious Quinn is much more appealing to me." My fingers rove him, exploring his build, remembering it. Damn. I feel like a miniature in this man's huge arms. Every inch of him is made of muscles standing boldly. Shoulders. Chest. Abdomen. Legs. Back. Fucking ass. I linger there, slipping a finger between the cheeks. They clench, but he doesn't stop feeling up my tits, the full length of his cock probing between my thighs.

Hot drops trickle from my pussy as he lowers his mouth to my areolas, suckling vigorously. When he's done with them, my nipples are engorged to the point of pain. He glances at me as he traces my skin with soft kisses down to my belly.

He holds my hip with one hand, the other parting my legs. Then he looks down. I like the way his eyes stay there. The way his tongue darts out as he does.

His hungry licks are impatient. His labored breaths have me in flames. My hands bury into his long hair, my breathing exerted, too.

Having a man who loves me is one thing, having one I love as well is…surreal. A level of intimacy that can't be replicated with anyone regardless of how good and experienced they are in satisfying my needs. I've been waiting for this intimacy for so long. A decade of seduction and games.

A torture Quinn and I both hate and crave.

It all ends now.

My eyes savor him, down on his knees, chained in a dingy cell, devouring my pussy, his erection hard and heavy. I pull his hair, forcing him to look at me, his lips and chin stained with my juices. "I should have made you my sex slave years ago."

"Majesty doesn't like slaves."

"I'm allowed to change my mind."

"I wish I had that luxury myself," he whispers, breaking.

I hear him. Loud and clear. A triumphant smile takes over me. "Get up."

He labors to his feet. I grab the chair and place it behind him. Then I push him, compelling him to sit.

Bracing myself for what's to come, I hold the back of the chair for support as I spread my legs and rest my thighs on his. My hand feels the length of his shaft, and he throbs with big twitches.

"I love you, Elysia." His voice trembles.

I love you, too.

My hands leave his cock and settle on his face. I lift myself and take him all inside me.

My lashes flutter, my lids shutting against my will. His groan vibrates through me, triggering my own sounds of pleasure.

I force my eyes open to delight in his expression, in his loving, surrendering eyes, my breaths painful in my chest, his breaths searing my face.

His grip squeezes my ass, kneading, as his pelvis thrusts upward against me. "I've been so stupid." He takes my lips between his. "So fucking stupid."

My belly undulates as I do a slow, torturous roll of my hips, encircling him. He cries out, clasping my waist, pushing harder against me.

"You still wish to die, Quinn?" I gasp for breath, fingernails spearing his flesh. "You still wish to leave me?"

"I never wished to leave you." His girth fills me with unprecedented, unstoppable pleasure. "I feel more of a fool now…that I actually know what I've been missing…making my stupid decisions, my Queen." He cries out louder. "I deserve to be punished even more."

His pace quickens, thrusts coming one upon the other. My hair shakes loose and my moans become indistinguishable from sobs. I make him feast on my tits as he drives me to the edge. A few more clenches and I writhe, lost in my own world. My crescendo inspires his own screams of climax.

I press him to my chest, absorbing his heat, his passion, enfolding him with my heart. As if it's too much for him to bear, Quinn lets go of his tears.

I've never seen a man cry this hard. A man who has lost everything. Regretted everything.

My eyes burn with emotions only he can evoke. "I pushed your execution day to apply the act of mercy without suspicion from the people. All you have to do is beg for it." My arms tighten around his weeping body.

The shackles chime as he wipes his face and lifts his head to me. A flicker of hope strikes his gaze, but it fades away the next moment. "Even if that's possible, what happens next, Majesty? I'll be banished, and I will never see you again. It's a destiny worse than death for me."

"At least, you'll live."

"Can't you see, my love? I don't want to live without you." He caresses my cheek with the back of his hand. "Can't live without you, Elysia."

My skin turns cold all of a sudden. "What are you telling me?"

His face contorts in anguish. "I'm telling you I regret making all the wrong choices, but sadly, nothing can make them right." He sniffles. "I'm very sorry."

Blinded by rage, I smack his face harder than I ever have I hear his neck crack. Then I get off him, but I cup my sex with one hand so that his seed won't spill. I use my other hand on his shoulder for support when I climb him. I balance my feet on his thighs and free my cunt, letting the thick cum drop on his face.

"Majesty!" He closes his eyes and his mouth in disgust and shock.

"Take that, you stupid bitch." I get down and find my dress.

"What was that for?" he mumbles, his face covered in the sticky liquid.

"For never learning." I reach inside the

191

pocket of my cloak, looking for my own set of keys to the shackles and the gate. "I own you, Quinn. Your body. Your heart. Your miserable life. All mine." Unchaining him, I look him in the eyes. "You will do as I say, whether you like it or not."

"Please understand me. I—"

"I don't want to hear it." I finish dressing myself and head for the door.

He grabs my hand. "Will I see you again...before the day?"

"Will you beg for mercy?"

He stares at me for a second, but he can't hold it for long.

"Goodbye, Sir." I yank my hand out of his grasp and stalk to the gate.

"Majesty," he calls as I turn the key into the lock.

My heart skips a beat. Hoping for a better ending to this encounter, I look at him over my shoulder.

"You forgot your cloak."

A chorus of curses flares inside my head. "Use it to wipe your cum off your ugly face, or better yet use it on your dick for release. This cloak is the closest thing you'll ever get to being with me again."

15.
THEODORE

"She's here! Her Majesty is here!" The boys' squeals drift faintly up to my chamber from downstairs.

I bolt upright, immediately in vertigo. Yet I swing my legs across the mattress until they dangle inches from the hardwood floor and prop my hands along the edge of the bed.

Soaking in cold sweat, I manage to get up. I drag my feet with all the strength left in me, lurching, heading for the door.

It opens before I reach, and I see her.

Beautiful and mighty as always.

Untouched by the agony swirling in the Royal land.

She looks at me as if she's seen a ghost. I might as well be. After that night, I haven't slept or eaten. An illness has taken over my soul before my body.

"Majesty." I attempt to smile as I reach to kiss her hand, but I fail to do both. As if all my power has been reserved to the moment I see her again.

The world spins. My legs wobble. The last thing I hear before I collapse is Her Majesty yelping my name.

16.
THEODORE

Fire and ice.

My eyes open to see them both in harmony.

The red hair flowing down Her Majesty's back as she watches through my window snow covering the ground.

The power of beauty and the power of destruction combined.

"Majesty," I whisper, shifting my weight on my elbows to sit up.

"Oh, Theo. Thank God." She hurries to sit next to me. Her hand touches my forehead as if checking my temperature, the other fixes a pillow behind my head. "Don't move. You're still sick."

Quickly, I adjust the pillow myself. Even if I'm ill, it's no excuse for me to stay still while my Queen assists. "How long have I been out?"

"Three days. You worried me sick. However, the physician assures me you're strong enough to recover from this."

I hold her hand and bring it to my lips. Then I place it on my heart. "Thank you, Majesty. I'm so glad you're here. I was losing my mind after that night."

"I'm terribly sorry, Theo. I never meant for you to get caught up in this chaos."

"I'm the one who should be sorry, Majesty, and I am. The guilt has been tearing me apart. I was hoping to see you…to make sure you're all right…to do anything to—"

Her finger touches my mouth, hushing me. "None of this is your fault."

"How could you say that, my Queen? I'm the one who…" My throat closes, and I feel like my soul is being ripped out of my chest. "A man is going to die because of what I did. Your man."

"You were following my orders." She strokes my hair softly. "If anything happens, it's on me. Only me."

My gaze roams her face, studying it. She speaks as if none of this matters. Her composure is beyond my understanding. How can she be so…aloof?

Her Majesty's passion is a force to reckon with. She's a creature made of strong, deep insatiable emotions with a heart as big as the ocean. How is it that she's this cold and detached when a man she loves to bits is

196

about to be executed?

"Why are you looking at me like this?" she asks.

I just stare at her for a few seconds. "You're scaring me."

"Not in a good way, I assume?"

I try to swallow, but my mouth is too dry. A wave of nausea washes over me. Is it illness or real fear? I'm not sure.

"I think I know why you're scared of me. You think I'm heartless, indifferent to what happens to Quinn."

"I know you're not. That's why I'm scared."

"Unlike what others might think, the Queen can't do however she pleases. *Feel* however she pleases. My emotions can't be revealed. They must remain under constant control even if I'm dying on the inside."

"But you're with me now, where you can be yourself. Elysia, the woman, not the Queen."

"I don't wish to lay more burdens on you, Theo. I've already damaged you enough." She squeezes my hand gently. "I'd rather take care of you now."

You're bluffing again, Majesty. It's either you're running away from your pain, trying to save me instead of him, or you have

something in your mind.
  A plan unrevealed.
  A dangerous one.

17.
HER MAJESTY

I've broken all my rules.

Built a harem of virgins. Driven a man to his demise. Fucked my escorts. Bent the strictest of my laws.

Sin after sin after sin…

It doesn't seem like the road to hell is going to end any time soon, either. I might as well repent my sorrow and indulge in more sins. More gleeful ones. Hopeful. Not bleak.

Break another tiny rule.

"Theo." I gaze at his pale face, his arctic eyes never more vibrant, his lips erotic red. Even in sickness, he's sensational. The corners of my mouth curve up as I remember him using the same word to describe me the first time we accidently touched.

"Yes, Majesty." He returns a bigger smile.

"I told you to call me by my name when we're alone."

"Of course." He prints a little kiss inside my palm. "Elysia."

"What is that you've always wanted from

me?" I don't waste any more time.

His eyes shimmer with surprise and joy, but then he blinks and glowers. "A kiss," he replies cautiously. "But you said you wouldn't do it because you wouldn't be able to feel it the way I wanted you to feel it. You wouldn't be able to reciprocate a fraction of the affection I showed you."

Goodness. He recalls my words verbatim.

"I know I told you that I'd rather delude myself that I might with time one day fall for you." I lean into him, gaze focused on his luscious lips. It's undeniable that I've always wanted to taste them. "It's not a delusion anymore."

"False hope," he reminds me. "You called it false hope."

"I think now is the most suitable time to put that hope to test to prove to you before me it's not false, either."

"Please don't." His plea, barely audible, stops me midway.

I retract and scrutinize his reaction, groping for the reason behind it. He glances up at me, almost in tears.

"I don't understand," I say.

"You don't love me, Elysia. Your heart belongs to him and him alone. You're only going to kiss me to drown your pain. A distraction, nothing more. This is too much cruelty for me to bear, and you've always said you didn't wish to hurt me like this...so please don't."

I chuckle.

His brows furrow. "You're amused?"

I wet my lips. "Do you think a woman can be in love with more than one man at the same time?"

"No, Majesty."

"I used to think the same. A woman can only share her body but never her heart." I shake my head. "Now I know it's not true."

"I beg to differ, my Queen. Your body is under your control. You may share it with whomever you wish because you can. But your heart... You can't control which way it beats."

"That's exactly why I know it can desire more than one man just like my body. My heart has beaten against my control. Against my logic. All logic."

"What?"

I rise, leaving his bed. "The boys have been practicing to perform for me. You're welcome to join. Some amusement will benefit you to heal faster."

"Elysia, don't run please. Is it true?"

"I'm not running. It's you who's afraid. I'm

not a fan of hesitation as you know."

"I'm not. I swear." He takes the sheets off him and gets out of the bed, his movements labored. "Please don't tell me I've missed my chance. Don't tell me I repeated *his* unwise mistake."

18.
THEODORE

My heart thrashes as her eyes pierce me. I can barely stand, but I will wait and never rest till the end of times if that's what it takes for her to forgive my ridiculous behavior.

To allow herself to love me.

To spare me a life of torment beyond redemption.

"The moment has passed," she finally says.

"No."

"Theodore, you're not well. I misjudged the timing. I shall go—"

I don't know how or what demon has possessed me at the moment, but my lips have just crushed hers.

She resists at the beginning, but I don't stop.

I won't stop.

My arms confine her tense body in an embrace, terrified to let go. Gradually, her mouth yields, and she goes limp in my grasp.

Then *I* dissolve in her kiss. The softness of

her lips. The swirl of her tongue. The passion of Elysia.

She kisses with such appetite that swallows a man whole, taking away all his resolve, stealing his heart along with his soul, chaining him to a life of sweet servitude.

Consensually.

She breaks the kiss and stares at me, her cherry lips swollen. I'm too lost in the moment to understand the penalties of what I've just done. My body, on the other hand, seems to comprehend them perfectly; I'm frozen, out of breath, and my heart is about to break my ribs with its pounding.

"Are you out of your mind?" she whispers.

"Apparently," I reply.

"Do you know how severely I will punish you?"

"It's worth it." My heart pounds harder at the insolence of the words flying out of my mouth. What the hell am I thinking?

I'm not.

She speaks the truth. I am out of my mind.

Anticipating what she will say next is like waiting for a death sentence. She knows how to intimidate, taking her time. Her silence and the way she looks at me send me shuddering.

Am I going to be physically tortured? Humiliated to her pleasure? Or am I going to wind up in a cell like Sir Quinlan, denied the honor of serving her ever again?

Please say it's the former. Please.

19.
HER MAJESTY

I love everything about this boy.

The purity of his emotions. The intensity of his fear. The strength of his heart. The beauty on the inside before the outside.

Perhaps I've been only attracted to him in the beginning because of the innocence and the virginity. The incredible physicality and the looks that remind me of Quinn.

But now I know Theodore is nothing like Quinn. The boy has more courage than that of the bravest of my guards.

I love him for it.

I truly do.

He's waiting for my sentence, thinking he's committed the worst crime possible. He doesn't know it's quite the opposite.

I'm not going to punish you, Theo. I'm going to reward you.

Theodore has won a piece of my heart that's going to be his forever.

A smile tugging at my mouth bids his

blood to run. "Do that again."

It takes him a second to recover and grin back. His hands secure my waist as he tastes my lips again, jolts of heat pulsing through me.

I pull away, full of desire and joy. His cheeks are no longer pale. His grip no longer faint. "You seem to have quite regained your strength all of a sudden."

"You have magic powers, Your Majesty. Your lips resurrect the dead."

A genuine laugh seeps out of me. I haven't laughed since that night at the solarium. "And yours can brighten the saddest of hearts."

A dark shadows crosses his bright eyes. "Are you really going to execute him?"

"He has left me no choice."

"There must be a way."

"Let me worry about that, Theo. I still have four days till the execution day. A lot can happen in four days."

20.
HER MAJESTY

Theo bathes and accompanies me to the theatre, where the rest of the boys, Claudius, James and Luke, are getting ready to perform their first play.

"Theodore, glad you could join us. Hope you're better now," Claudius says from the stage.

"I feel quite rejuvenated, thank you." Theo kisses my hand and ushers me to the front row. I sit and allow him a seat next to me. "So what are we watching?" he asks me.

"Romeo and Juliet...with a twist. There's nothing better to entertain than a fine piece of literature altered to suit our own fantasies."

"But it's a tragedy."

"Not in my version." My eyes wander to the three boys on the stage, all bare-chested, carved to perfection. Their bodies are oiled, and every hair has been removed so that the muscles are magnified. The generous length and girth of their cocks, though veiled under pants, are visible, hanging heavily between their thighs.

They're all blond except for Claudius. He reminds me of a certain black man Sir Connor has once brought to my playroom. A brat who likes it rough with the most perfect ass I've ever seen. The memory alone makes my *mouth* water. I chuckle to myself. What is it with black men that grabs a woman's attention and leaves a mark never forgotten?

"We're ready when Your Majesty is," Claudius says.

I nod. "By all means."

The lights glare. The boys' skins glisten under them. The performance starts.

"Did you know your fellow Temple boys like to play with each other?" I whisper in Theo's ear.

"Play?" he wonders.

"Yes. Degenerate queer play," I mock, chortling.

He scowls. "No, Majesty. I wasn't aware."

"You live under the same roof and you've never seen or heard them…fornicate?"

He stares at me with utter shock, and then his stare shifts toward the boys. "Fornicate?"

"You should know I don't mind if you, too, like to play with them."

His head whips back in my direction. "No."

"It's all right. You can tell me."

"In all seriousness, I really don't like or wish to…play…with boys. Ever."

"Fine. I must advise you that if you're uncomfortable with watching this kind of performance as well, you're free to leave."

"You mean they're about to… Live?"

I grin. "In my version, Mercutio, Tybalt and Benvolio all have their way with each other. Juliet gets Romeo as well as all the other boys. No one dies. They all live happily ever after."

Astonishment escalates upon his face. "Do you like to watch boys together?"

I shrug. "I might. I haven't seen it before."

He runs a hand through his raven hair. "You never fail to shock me, my Queen."

21.
THEODORE

Her Majesty's head rests on my shoulder, our arms linked as I watch my former companions of holiness, now my partners in sin, writhe in more sinful pleasures.

Claudius is the first to undress. He parades his body for Her Majesty with earned swagger. The ebony giant's masculinity is remarkable. I'm certain I'm not the sole man in the room who envies him.

Luke and James practice in soft dalliances, touching and kissing each other, their eyes not meeting, though, focused only on our woman.

Our chosen goddess.

Unlike what she might think—despite their evident joviality—they aren't performing for their own gratification. They're doing it for her. The way they look at her proves it.

It's not long before the other two stand nude. Claudius huge hands bend Luke over and grasp his buttocks, and he begins the slow rubbing of his shaft along the crease.

James drops to his knees, settling himself into a comfortable position before them, touching himself, his eyes smoldering.

Her Majesty's hand slips under my shirt, traveling my skin, absentmindedly. I notice how she wets her lips, how her eyes glaze with arousal as the black mountain of a man continues his labors behind, heavy testicles bumping against Luke's own with each motion.

Then James begins his feast. He takes Luke's cock into his mouth.

My stomach flips. This is wrong. Unnatural.

I'm fully aware that I'm in no place to judge—I'm covered in sin from head to toe—but male cock sucking and ass fucking are not scenes I wish to witness, let alone enjoy. I should leave, but my legs won't move, tied by invisible chains. I feel if I go, she will be disappointed in me. She likes a man who takes risks, who's not afraid of breaking the rules.

For her.

She lifts her head and takes her hand off me. "You're so tense. I can tell you're having a hard time watching. You may go back to your room and rest."

"No, Majesty. If it pleases you, it pleases me." I drag my gaze back to the stage, determined to steel myself for whatever Her Majesty has in mind. A surge of arousal at the control she wields over me springs my dick to life.

Her hand refuses to stay idle for a second. It grabs my penis with urgency. I shift in my seat, swallowing.

She touches my cheek and leans in to my ear, so close that her hair brushes my lobe. "Are you too sick to be touched?"

"By you? Never." Her strokes make me swallow again. "I really missed you, Elysia. More than you think."

She gives me one of her most charming, flirtatious, crooked smiles. "I will join the boys in a few minutes. Perhaps you wish to participate, too."

22.
HER MAJESTY

Theo's cock stiffens in my fist. Is it only my touch that's causing the firm response? Or is it his heart's rapid beat—out of fear or excitement or both—that fuels the erection?

As my hand slithers under his pants, now rubbing the velvet skin itself, his ragged breaths join those coming from the stage.

I sigh, the throbbing in my pussy unbearable, my rubbing quicker, my gaze pinned to the naked boys. There can be no doubt that James's enjoyment matches Luke's. He grasps the back of Luke's thighs, pulling him deeper into his throat. Such vigor in the suction of his mouth is executed as if entirely for his own pleasure.

His hands move from the back of Luke's thighs to his balls, cupping them tightly while his mouth plunges. Luke thrusts forward with natural inclination.

The dark cock moves more easily now. I assume the movements have lubricated it in its confinement.

"Majesty, our Juliet, please join us now. I'm on the edge of my control," Luke says, his voice strained with arousal.

Slowly, I move away from Theo, planting a little kiss on his cheek, then stand.

"You're serious about leaving me like this?" He points at his crotch with both hands, his chest rising and falling with each breath.

I tease him with a smile as I head to the naughty boys. "You may finish the job yourself if you wish."

He shakes his head in disbelief, and I giggle.

James leaves Luke's cock to help me up. It remains full-veined and potent at full extension. James's penis may not be as hard, but it will be very soon. "Fair Juliet, allow us to serve your darkest whims of desire."

I giggle louder. "Oh boy, you do not wish to know about those darkest whims."

He bows, swallowing as he realizes what I'm referring to. "Of course." He kisses my hand and twirls me into a waltz. "Nonetheless, we have certain delicacies on the menu that Majesty might find appealing."

Claudius is about to stop, but I nod at him to continue while I move with James's arms. "Such as?"

"Tit massage aperitif." His fake accent makes me chortle. "Pussy-licking fit for royalty for an entrée."

"Ménage-a-quatre for the main course," Luke adds, groaning from the thrusts up his ass. Then he looks at Theo, our single audience. "Cinque, perhaps, to suit Juliet's appetite."

Waltzing, pressing James's semi-erection and naked body to mine, I laugh my heart out. "Theo is for dessert."

"He's always the lucky one." Claudius wraps one mighty arm around Luke's abdomen, drawing him close to his own, and reaches around with the other hand, taking the root of the his penis in his grip. Thumb and forefinger form a tight circumnavigation of its girth, while the remaining fingers brush the front of Luke's testicles.

"Oh God," Luke gasps. "Majesty, may I come?"

"In a minute. I'm a little overdressed for the show."

"Let me take care of that, dear Juliet." James stops the dance and takes his time undressing me. "May I serve your aperitif now?" he asks when he frees my breasts. "Pretty please?"

"You're so naughty." I swirl my index

finger in the air, commanding him to turn.

He bows his head as if embarrassed and obeys. I ogle his little white ass before I spank it with hard swats. The feeling of my palm against the heat of his butt cheeks makes me wet. "I prefer to have my aperitif and entrée at the same time."

I push the dress down and step out of it, stealing a quick glance at Theo. His posture is more relaxed. His eyes are glistening. He's better enjoying the show now.

James grabs a padded chair and gestures for me to sit. I order him to move it closer to Luke.

When I sit, I part my legs, ready to be served. I kiss James as his hands fondle my tits, and Luke's mouth eats my hot vulva, his guttural sounds inspired by Claudius big black cock resonate inside me.

"Majesty, please allow me to come," Luke beseeches me.

"Claudius, have you entered him yet?" An erotic tingling travels through my body and swells between my thighs.

"Not yet. I'm just knocking at his door."

"Stop knocking and come open my female portal."

Claudius lets go of Luke's hips and exits him with a moan. He walks toward me, his engorged dick staring at my face. "At your command, *Juliet*. We're all here to please you."

"Luke, it's your turn to fuck this gorgeous black ass. You may come there." I caress Claudius's ass myself.

His eyebrows arch. "So Luke fucks me, and I…"

I bite my lips. "Fuck me."

He blows out a long breath. "This is incredibly arousing."

"Not fair, Majesty. What does that leave me?" James grumbles, his massage ongoing.

"You have my tits, bitch. Touch, suck or fuck. Play all you want. Touch yourself all you want." I get off the chair and use some of the boys' clothes as sheets below me when I lie down on my back.

The three boys get in position, Claudius on top of me, Luke on top of him and James on my side.

The dark hands start a sensual worship of my body, not that I need more stimulation. I crush the thick lips into mine to show him I'm done being teased. My fist guides the giant to my center. "Fuck me now."

He swims inside my wetness, stretching my pussy, filling me to the maximum, James flicking my nipple with his tongue.

"Now, Luke. Don't just knock on his

door." I moan, Claudius's thrusts clench my pussy faster than I anticipate.

The pressure doubles when Luke starts. My eyes search for Theo's , and when I see that he's watching with eagerness, the strength of spasms in my sex overwhelms me.

This is so fucking good. The ménage. The male on male action. The watching. "Are you having as much fun as I am, Luke?"

"Yes, Majesty. My wet penis is pressing solidly at his door. Stop struggling, Claudius and let me in."

"Oh dear God," Claudius groans heavily, the rhythmic grinding against me fast. "Would that please you, Juliet?"

"So-o-much."

"Fine. After all, there's a thrill in the charge of a hot cock nudging at my rear. Do it, Luke. Pleasure our goddess."

The Adonis pushes inside me while Luke inches within. Their roars of arousal intersect.

I lift James's head off my chest, pausing the suckling for a moment, and press his red lips to mine. His shaft pokes my side, begging for attention. I squeeze him in my grasp, which fuels the fire in my belly.

Theo is now on his feet, approaching slowly, the bulge in his pants clear from my view.

"Speed up, boys. Let's make a very big mess." I gasp for breath, certain the erection in my palm is about to burst. "Come now, Luke."

"May I climax, too, Majesty?" Claudius sweats.

"Yes!" My own climax is imminent. "And when you hear him come, James, you come in his face."

"Fuck... Yes, Majesty, as you wish," James complies.

Luke steadies his grip and thrusts deeper, shooting his abundance. Claudius slumps forward, his knees weak, held up by the man behind him. Then I feel his ejaculate throbbing through me.

"Now, James!" I yell.

The blond's seed arches in Claudius's face.

This final act along with Theo's voracious gaze orchestrate my screams of orgasm.

As the four of us recover from the force of release, Theo jumps on the stage, as if he were never ill. "Is there room for dessert, dear Juliet?"

23.
HER MAJESTY

I smile lazily at Theo. "Always."

"Allow me to cleanse your palette first," James offers.

Luke and Claudius leave the scene to clean themselves, while James cleans my pussy with his tongue. He licks Claudius's cum like a hungry animal, unashamed.

"Filthy cuckold." I chortle.

He smiles up at me. "Aren't we all?"

I grin, enjoying him licking and sucking every drop out of my cunt. After he's done, I get up and saunter toward Theo, who's undressed, sitting in the chair. I marvel at the beauty I've long missed. The first of my harem. The ending of my starvation. The beginning of a different era of lust and sinful impulses.

Settling on top of him has never been more rewarding. Taking another cock right after a heavy climax is intense. The nerves in my pussy are stinging still, feeling everything with heightened sensations.

"Am I Romeo in your version?" Theo starts with a slow motion.

"One of the three Romeos." My fingers twine behind his neck.

"Three?" His eyes narrow. "Who's the third? Don't tell me Sir Edward, too, has drunken the love potion?"

I push myself down on him, matching his tempo. "Sir Edward swallowed that potion years ago. It's I who's gulping on it these days."

He shakes his head, his fingers digging my ass. His strokes take a heated beat.

Angry jealous sex. I love it.

"James, do you want to come again while watching us?" I ask, knowing Theo will get angrier.

"Thank you, Majesty. Yes." The blond rubs himself instantly.

Theo growls, thrusting harder, his hands squeezing my flesh to the point of pain. I don't stop him. I need the roughness.

"You were right, Majesty. If in less than a week, Sir Edwards pisses on his bond with his long life friend and jumps into your bed, a lot can happen in four days," he says with effort, his breath catching.

"I'm counting on it." My pussy tightens around him, and after a few more strokes, we both find our release. Our voyeur follows with equal passion.

24.
QUINN

One Day to Execution

Wrapped in filth and her red cloak, I lie on the floor, awaiting death. Tomorrow everything ends. Whatever I choose to do, my life as I know it concludes.

Footsteps approach, and my hearts leaps. Has Her Majesty decided to revisit her old slave? Will she grant a dying man his last wish?

My hopes are thwarted when I see Edward coming forth.

A friendly face to comfort me before my demise.

"It took you long enough," I say as he enters the cell.

"Her Majesty's orders." He sweeps my confinement with his eyes before he closes the gate.

I purse my lips. "Of course."

"How have you been?" He barely looks at me.

I chuckle a humorless laugh. "Not so much different than I've been out there. In her service, I've always been a dead man walking or a dead man crawling."

"You can start over. She's been kind enough to give you one last chance."

"Kind?" I shout incredulously. "That is such a ridiculous word to describe our Queen, dear friend. She's evil. Every cell in her is sinful."

"And we are without sin?"

I look away. "Why are you here, Edward? Or should I ask why she's sent you?"

"She wishes to know your final decision. She doesn't want any surprises tomorrow."

"She thinks you can persuade me to beg for mercy?"

He shrugs. "Apparently."

"Is she really that keen on saving *my sorry ass*?"

"What do you think, you stupid fuck?"

I hear something in his voice. Something bitter and angry. Now I sweep his face, his expression hard to read. No compassion, reproach or sorrow. No eye contact either.

Something is different about Edward.

"Are you all right, brother?" I ask.

"Like hell I am." He spins on his heels and crouches down. His eyes finally settle on mine. "But don't you dare pretend you care. You're a fucking coward who only cares about himself."

"What?" I stare back, shocked, a nauseated feeling in my stomach. "What are you... That's her words, not yours. Why are you speaking like her...brother?"

"You didn't just leave her, you left me, too. You never thought about the agony you'd be causing both of us. You just ran, threw yourself over a cliff to end your miserable life while we suffer your mess. I share Her Majesty's vision now."

"No." Blood pumps through my veins with frightening speed. My palms itch, and I want to slam his head into the wall and then reach down his throat and pull his heart out through his mouth. "You share her bed."

His head lowers before he straightens and gives me his back.

"You don't even make the effort to deny it. Is that why you're really here? To rub it in my face? Did she tell you to do it so she'd torture me some more?"

"You're unbelievable. You think everything is about you." He growls, facing me again. "I'm here to tell you that your treason led to consequences that could ruin our Queen...brother."

"What consequences? What the hell is going on?" I raise my voice.

"You think people are stupid? They will believe this Holiday season charade? What do you think they're whispering among each other, spreading rumors about the reason behind what you did?"

"No one dares speak ill of my Queen," I hiss.

"That was before, genius."

"I never thought—"

"That your actions could impact us all? Well, it did. Yet she doesn't care. She is bending the law for you without the slightest concern what people will say about her because she fucking *loves* you," he spits. "So the least you can do is obey, you asshole, and live."

I've been blind for so long.

By my ego.

And my love for her.

I am selfish as they say. A coward, too.

Taking a deep, sharp breath, I muse at the past decade in a moment of clarity. "You once told me as long as you were there, serving her, nothing else mattered to you. You were thankful and satisfied."

"Yes. I still am."

"I know now you're absolutely right. I

regret not understanding this from the start."

He stares at me, fear striking his eyes. "You still have a chance at this life, Quinn. Don't waste it, please."

"I have already made up my mind, Ed."

"Please say I should tell Her Majesty you are going to beg for mercy tomorrow."

I take one last glance at him. My hands, reflexively, wrap the cloak tighter around my shoulders. "Tell her I won't live a life without her."

"Quinn—"

"Goodbye, brother. I wish you all the happiness there is."

25.
HER MAJESTY

Execution Day

A black gown.
Quietly, the maids assist me put it on. The red shades of my hair glare against my pale skin and dark attire.

The festive decorations that have colored the kingdom haven't touched the Royal land. In here, everything is black like my dress and white as the snow piling on the grounds.

I stare at my reflection in the full length mirror before me, spiraling in my own thoughts, demons thriving in my anguish as if it's not enough that I'm looking one in the face right now.

One of the maids places on my head the final touch of this sick portrait. The crown. "Do you need anything else, Majesty?" Her voice is sad like everything about today.

I don't know if she, like the rest of my people, is unhappy for me or cursing me in her head. Sometimes I doubt everyone knows what has happened between me and Quinn, sees the true colors of their ruler.

I glance at her, looking for an answer in vain. "Thank you. You may be dismissed."

Edward enters as they leave, bringing the endless rambling in my head to a temporary halt. "It's time, Your Majesty," he announces.

"He's been transferred to the Justice House safely?"

"Yes. The guards confirm that he's delivered in one piece."

I nod, but my feet refuse to move. "There's no escaping today, isn't it?"

He shakes his head slowly. "I fear not."

"I've done everything that I could to save him." I struggle to keep my voice steady.

"I don't doubt it, my Queen."

"He's not going to do it." Pain squeezes in my chest. "He will make me kill him."

"Despite what he said, there are signs that he's clinging to life still. He hasn't taken his own life and he was holding to Your Majesty's cloak like a second skin." He approaches me. "I believe there's still hope."

"We shall know shortly." I nod again, filling my lungs with air. "Let's go. There's no point delaying the inevitable."

We leave and ride the designated chariot to the execution arena—a courtyard outside the Justice House. The masses have already gathered. As the guards pave the way for me to pass, I inspect some of the people's faces. They're filled with pity and sorrow unlike the livid, heated expressions I've always met in an occasion such as this.

Quinn is loved, indeed.

His tragedy has touched every house in the realm.

I wonder when he dies today, are they going to blame me for it? Will they curse the Laws of the Vow? Will they call me a heartless bitch?

As I pass through, bows and curtsies flank the path. The faces don't change when they see me. Except they soften as if they're...consolidating me.

Can they see the pain underneath the pride? Can they see the hurt masked by the power?

Can they see my heart?

I climb the stone steps and reach my seat, a throne-like chair padded with red velvet, in a gallery prepared in front of the entrance of the Justice House, Edward by my side, Chief of Ministers awaiting.

When I sit, I take another look at the people and Edward before I gesture at Chief to commence.

He recites the crime of Sir Quinlan according to the Laws of the Vow and states the verdict followed by the sentence.

Execution with no chance for mercy.

Roars rumble from the crowds. I hear the word mercy resonating in multiple voices and pitches. Chief looks at me, and I nod my assent to declare what we've agreed upon.

"In the spirit of the Holiday season and all its benevolence, Her Majesty has been kind and generous enough to grant the people before the traitor a gift to brighten this holy time of the year. Let it always be merry and never bleak.

"Her Majesty, with your sanction, good people of the realm, would offer Quinlan the traitor a chance for mercy," he concludes.

"Yes!"

"Thank you, Majesty!"

"Please! Yes! He doesn't deserve to die!"

"Sir Quinlan is not a traitor!"

These cries and similar ones dominate the arena and rise upon a few disapproving voices.

"The people have spoken, Your Majesty," Chief says.

I inhale, pressing my hands together. "Thank you. On the authority of the crown, I declare the act of mercy valid today."

The crowds boom with joy and relief.

Unlike me, they don't know all this is for

nothing. Quinn won't beg for mercy. I know him better than anyone.

The executioner arrives, clad in a leather hood, and ascends to his station of pain and death, carrying a wrap under his arm. He sets it on the table and unfolds the wrapped piece of cloth, revealing the torturing tools. Knives, saws, nail clippers…

Devices even I won't enjoy.

Not today.

All eyes are on me now. There's nothing left to begin but my order. The command that will bring Quinn to his ending.

I lift my chin up to avoid the tears forming behind my eyelids. "Bring him out."

The guards' steps bang in my ears, but my heart unsystematic beat is louder. I press my fist to my mouth, dying in every second of waiting a thousand times.

Why haven't they brought him yet? I don't wish to stay in this day any longer. I want it over so I can mourn and grieve him.

So this unbearable pain leaves me alone.

This is taking too long.

Longer than it should.

Chief, Edward and I are staring at the entrance, but no one is showing.

I look from Chief to Edward. "Something isn't right. What's happening?"

"I'll go check," Chief stalks to the doors, but the guards emerge.

They scurry with panic on their expressions. As they reach Chief, they say something that blanches his face.

My heart skips a beat.

He spins and walks toward me with the slowest, smallest steps ever.

"Speak, Chief of Ministers. What happened?!"

"He's dead," he states almost inaudibly but the words pelt my ears. "Quinlan poisoned himself."

I rise from my seat, my legs too numb to carry me. Then everything goes black.

26.
EDWARD

The Temple mourning bells announce the death of Quinn official.

It's not a bad dream from which I will sober. It's real. The worst nightmare.

My friend has died.

My Queen is unawake.

I am here, standing guard at her door for hours.

Alone.

Without hope. As good as dead.

A thoughtless note in my pocket fetched from the red cloak.

His suicide note.

The bloody words narrate in my head while the physician works his miracles on Her Majesty.

The last of his updates informs me he's done everything to revive her, still she won't wake. A few hours later, the doors to her chamber open behind me, and he tells me there's nothing else to do but wait.

Wait? What does that even mean?

I enter. The room is dark. The maids surround her, weeping, dressed in black like angels of death. My Queen lies peacefully in her bed, her hands placed on top of her chest. "What the hell is this?" I reach her bed, glaring at the maids. "Turn on more lights and leave us."

They glance at each other hesitantly.

"Now," I bark.

They run and do as commanded.

I grab a chair and sit next to her, her bloodless face morbid. "Are you leaving me too, my Queen? Is that what you want?" The back of my hand brushes her cold cheek. "You, too, won't live a life without him? Is that what it is?"

My brain rejects this nonsense. She is the Queen. She has a son and thousands of people who love her.

She has her bastard who worships her.

She has me.

How can she leave all that for one man? She can't be that weak.

Can't be that cruel.

"Wake up, Elysia." I press my hands in a silent prayer. "You have to wake up, my love. For me. For all of us. Can't you see? We can't live without you."

Her body remains limp. Silence wraps my

heart. The gods won't answer a sinful man such as me.

I fish Quinn's note out of my pocket and read it aloud. Perhaps she will hear it. Perhaps his voice can bring her back.

"Forgive me, Your Majesty. I've chosen to take my own life to spare you the pain of watching me betraying you again. I've carried with me the bottle of poison since the day I stepped down from your service, knowing that your kind heart will do everything in its might to spare my life.

"I am a coward that chooses death over living in shame, banished from home, and a proud fool who won't let the people see him beg. I certainly don't deserve your mercy. But I do beg for your forgiveness.

"So mourn me not. I belong to oblivion. Though, I wish you would remember me in your prayers." I lift my head heavenwards, breaking in tears. Then my eyes fall on the signature, and I cry harder.

For Her Majesty.
Yours forever
Quinlan

"See? He didn't blame you. He only wanted your forgiveness and for you not be sad." I sniffle and touch her beautiful hair. "He loved you, Majesty. We all do."

A commotion erupts outside the door. Swiftly, I wipe my face and exits to see who dares disrupt Her Majesty.

I unsheathe my sword and barge out of Her Majesty's quarters doors. The bastard and his Temple boys stare me in the face.

"What the hell are you doing here?" I grind my teeth together.

The bastard steps forward and squares his shoulders. "We've come to see Her Majesty. We heard she's sick."

"You don't have the right to be here. Go back to your house before I kill you all." I wave my sword.

He takes another step toward me without an ounce of fear in his eyes. "We have every right to be here. She's our Queen, too."

"You will see her only when she wakes and wishes to visit you. Now go back where you came from because I won't ask again," I say with my strictest menacing tone.

One of the boys stands next to the bastard. "She needs us, Sir Edward. She needs to feel us all around her. Perhaps that's what brings her back."

"Please." The bastard's bright eyes beseech me.

Desperate as I am, it doesn't take me long to break the rules and allow them in. Perhaps they're right. I need all the help I can get.

All five of us gather around her bed, our hands joined in another prayer. The gods might be more merciful with their former servants than they are with me.

27.
THEODORE

The longest day in the history of the kingdom has ended at last. The early rays of dawn seep quietly through the windows and onto her calm, unchanging visage.

Heartache to heartache, we continue our prayers in her ears and in silence, united with one hope, never giving up.

"We're nothing without you, Elysia," I whisper, resting my head beside hers on her pillow, holding her hand, Sir Edward doing the same on the other side, the boys kneeling by the bed. "I'm sorry I'm calling you by your name when we're not alone. So wake up and punish me. Please." I raise her hand to my mouth for a kiss. "We're all here for you. Don't leave us alone."

"I guess her version of Romeo and Juliet was too optimistic to come true," Claudius says. "It has turned into a tragedy after all."

"Don't be too greedy, my Queen. Two Romeos can be enough, and they're here by your side at your disposal." Luke rubs his bloodshot eyes. I'm sure mine are more irritated and swollen.

"How about we kiss her?" James suddenly suggests.

"What?" Sir Edward lifts his head off the pillow, glaring at him.

"We each give her a kiss. Let her feel us closely. Let her sense how much we all love her. How much we need her."

I nod. "That's not a bad idea since we've run out of ideas, Sir Edward."

He closes his eyes, shrugging in resignation. "Fine."

The three boys start one by one, printing their kisses on her pale lips, Sir Edward and I not leaving her hands. Then my turn comes.

I put all the emotions in my heart in that kiss along with the hope and sincerity in wishing for her return. My hand squeezes her. "Please, Elysia. Plea…"

A gasp escapes my chest as my head jerks to her hand. "I felt something." My gaze travels among the rest of the men. "Her fingers moved inside my grasp."

Sir Edward bolts upright, and the boys jump and surround us closely.

"Do it, Sir Edward. Kiss her," I request eagerly.

His lips touch hers in a solemn reunion. His tears drop on her face. "Are you really awaking, my Queen?"

Her eyes move under their lids.

"Did you see that?"

"Yes!"

"Thank you, dear God."

The boys squeal like children. Sir Edward's chest and mine heave whilst we monitor Her Majesty, anticipating her next gesture.

Finally, she opens her eyes. Her faint squeezes inside my hand bring me back to life.

"Someone call for the physician," Sir Edwards demands.

"Ed," she murmurs.

"I'm here." He leans in, touching her forehead. "We're all here."

Her tired gaze wanders around all of our faces. Tears stream down her cheeks and drift into her mouth. "Take me to him."

28.
HER MAJESTY

Escorted by the five men who have given themselves to me and never faltered or given up, I travel to the Quinlan's corpse.

The coffin is blue and gray like the body inside, forsaken in the Chamber of Death in the deepest hole of the dungeon, where traitors like my former protector are processed for burial.

"Where's the cloak?" I ask.

Ed looks at me, puzzled.

I grasp the coffin for support, my legs weak. "You said he was clinging to the cloak like a second skin. Where is it?"

"You're looking at it, Majesty. In the coffin, under his head. He told one of the guards who brought him to the Justice House that if he died, he wished it'd be buried with him."

Still dazed from losing consciousness for almost a day, I take a second look. There is something under Quinn's long hair, but it's not red. I reach for it and carefully remove it without disturbing the peace of the dead.

When I touch it, I recognize it is in fact my cloak but so dirty and used that it's no longer red.

"What is so special about this cloak, Majesty?" Theo asks.

"You'll see." My fingers unfold the fabric and dip inside the pocket.

"It's where I found the note," Ed mumbles.

"You didn't find anything else?" I search along the edges of the pocket.

"No, Majesty. Are you looking for something in particular?"

My fingers still, and a small smile makes its way to my face. "I found it." I point at a slightly bulged spot on the thick fabric. "Here. Rip it."

Ed tears the cloth in half with one move, revealing a tiny, dark bottle shorter than a knuckle. He grabs it suspiciously. "What is this?"

I wave for him to give it to me.

He hands it over, arching a brow. "Majesty, what are you up to? You left the cloak in Quinn's cell on purpose, didn't you?"

Opening the bottle, I order, "Boys, go secure this chamber. I don't want anyone come near here until I'm finished."

James, Luke and Claudius scatter to secure the doors. Ed and Theo narrow their eyes at me, swallowing in anticipation.

My heart thuds against my ribs. Now, is a moment of truth, when everything goes as planned or the last of my hopes is murdered. Slowly, I lift Quinn's head and place the bottle on his mouth, making sure the dark liquid goes inside till the last drop.

Then I kiss him.

"Majesty, what are you doing?" Theo inquires, his voice intense.

My exhausted gaze doesn't leave Quinn. "My lips resurrect the dead."

"Majesty, that was a—"

A wild gasp interrupts him.

From the mouth I've just touched.

"Sweet heavens." Theo stumbles backwards.

"Holy fuck!" Edward runs both hands through his hair, holding his head.

I hear the three boys curse from here.

A jolt of ecstasy bursts through me as Quinn sits up, his eyes sparkling with life. "You finally made the right choice."

His cold lips press into mine. "I told you I wouldn't live a life without you."

"I hate to disturb this demonic reunion, but

could someone explain what the fuck is going on here?" Edward barks.

29.
QUINN

The Day Her Majesty Visited

"Use it to wipe your cum off your ugly face, or better yet use it on your dick for release. This cloak is the closest thing you'll ever get to being with me again." Her Majesty closes the cell behind her and leaves without looking back.

I wipe my face with the back of my hands and bang the walls with my fists, cursing the day I was born.

Cursing the day I met her.

What the fuck have I done to myself?

I kick the stupid cloak off the floor in a feeble attempt to make this fury blazing inside me fade. I stomp on it and desecrate it with the rest of my cum.

Then I feel it under my foot. Something in the pocket.

A piece of paper and a bottle.

Unfolding the note, I curl up in the corner to read.

Dear Quinn,

I have no doubt you won't beg for mercy. You're too arrogant for that. I can assure you this is not what I truly ask of you.

I came to you today to show you a glimpse of what we can have if you, for once, listen. I came here to save you. From death. From yourself.

With this note, you'll find a bottle. Drink it when you reach the Justice House. It will kill you.

My brows furrow as I look at the poison in my hand.

Yes, it will, but only temporarily. It's poison that reduces your bodily functions and faints your heartbeat almost to a halt as if you were dead. It's fake death, however. You will wake in less than a day.

Then there's another bottle. The antidote. You'll need it even if you've awaken on your own to live without complications. It's in a secret pocket in the same cloak. I leave it here in case something happens to me or I'm detained from giving it to you on time. Nonetheless, I'll make sure to be the first face you see when you're revived.

My fingers search hungrily for the secret pocket. I locate it with difficulty, but I find it.

The plan is to let the people think you're dead so I can have you all to myself with no judgment or fear.

No earthly consequences.

But you must know I'm not a woman for one man. If you choose to take this last chance I give you, be certain you're not going to be the only man in my life.

Only when you can let go of your pride and understand the nature of my love for you, we can be together.

Our happily ever after is not out of reach.

I don't wish to lose you, and I'm risking everything for you, Quinn.

My sweet Quinn.

I really hope you will make the right choice this time.

Yours truly,

Elysia

30.
QUINN

"I'm so sorry, Edward. I couldn't risk telling you that night. You had to react naturally so the people would believe." I step out of the coffin and hold his shoulders.

"I thought you were fucking dead. I've been going mad over losing you for a week. I've been mourning you for hours." He pushes my hands off him. "And you, Majesty, you knew he'd go through with it all along? You falling ill like this was all a charade?"

"No," she answers. "I had no idea this idiot was going to listen."

"You must thank Edward for that. When I knew you and he are…" I clench my teeth.

"More jealousy?" Her eyes reproach me.

"No, I promise. No more of that. I know my place now. I meant when I understood that you were giving both of us a chance to be a part of your…family," my pride forbids me from saying harem, "it settled it for me." I glance at Edward sideways. "You saved me, brother. I'm forever thankful."

His jaw flexes, his lips tight. "Don't thank me. Thank Her Majesty. I didn't know it then, but I'm certain it was all a part of her plan to send me over at that time."

"And the sickness?" the bastard shrieks. "We thought you were going to die."

"The cook must taste it. I drank the same poison only with less precipitation," she confesses. "I needed to know if it was going to work and convince the people I was devastated."

"Oh, love. You never said anything about that in the note. Elysia, no one is worth risking your life," I blame her.

"I told you I was risking everything for you, and it worked." She sighs in relief. "Speaking of the note, where is it?"

"Don't worry. I ate it. I wrote one of my own when I arrived at the Justice House to make the suicide more convincing to the people."

"Good boy." She chortles.

"Am I the only one who thinks this is pure insanity?" The bastard throws his hands in the air. "Where is he going to live? How are you going to see him, Majesty? How can we even get him out of here without getting recognized?"

She examines my face with a charming smile on her lips. "Quinn will live with you in the Art House."

"What?" he shrieks again. Foul words swirl from the doors.

"Like every royal house in the world, there are underground tunnels for emergencies in this one. They are located under this very dungeon, and they lead to various locations on the Royal land, including the Art House."

"But how can he live among us? What if he's spotted?"

"Even though I love it, he will cut his hair." She touches my hair, and I'm desperate to feel those fingers all over me. "Change his looks with makeup, the same kind previous residents of the Art House used." She turns to the bastard. "It's a bit extreme, but it will do for now. I trust you and the boys will take good care of him there?"

He lets out a long breath. "As you wish, Majesty. I can never disobey you."

"I hate you right now, for everything you've put us through." Edward looks at me as if I were the devil.

"I apologize again, but, brother, I'm alive. And we're all going to be living happily together. Isn't that what matters in the end?"

"I guess," he grumbles.

I open my arms and grab him into an embrace. He yields in the end and hugs me back. "I fucking missed you, asshole."

"I missed you, too." I pull away, looking in the eyes of my Queen. "And I missed you more than anything in the world."

She kisses me, and then she kisses them all.

I still have no idea how I'm going to do this. Live in hiding with men I don't like. Watch her with them.

Be someone else, completely different from who I am.

But I'm willing to learn.

For Her Majesty.

Always and forever.

GET MORE

Thanks for Reading!

N. J. Adel, the author of All the Teacher's Pets, Her Royal Harem, Seratis and I Hate You then I Love You series, is a cross genre author. From chocolate to books and book boyfriends, she likes it DARK and SPICY.

Bikers, rock stars, dirty Hollywood heartthrobs, smexy guards and men who serve. She loves it all.

She is a loather of cats and thinks they are Satan's pets. She used to teach English by day and write fun smut by night with her German Shepherd, Leo. Now, she only writes the fun smut.